THE
MYSTERY AT
NUMBER 31,
NEW INN

R. AUSTIN FREEMAN

JOURNEY FORTH™

Greenville, South Carolina

Library of Congress Cataloging-in-Publication Data

Freeman, R. Austin (Richard Austin), 1862-1943.
 [Mystery of 31, New Inn,]
 The mystery at number 31, New Inn / by R. Austin Freeman.
   p. cm.
 ISBN 1-59166-306-7 (perfect bound pbk. : alk. paper)
 1. Thorndyke, Doctor (Fictitious character)—Fiction. 2. Inheritance
and succession—Fiction. 3. London (England)—Fiction. 4. Physi-
cians—Fiction. I. Title.
   PR6011.R43M97 2004
   823'.912—dc22

                                                    2004014819

The Mystery at Number 31, New Inn

Design by C. Dailey Crafton
Cover photo © 2004 Brand X Pictures
Composition by Melissa Matos

© 2004 BJU Press
Greenville, SC 29614

15 14 13 12 11 10 9 8 7 6 5 4 3 2 1

PUBLISHER'S NOTE

British author Richard Austin Freeman (1862-1943) was a capable medical doctor whose knowledge of medicine and interest in scientific methods found a literary outlet in his mystery novels featuring Dr. John Thorndyke. Vital clues in *The Mystery at Number 31, New Inn* come from Freeman's broad base of knowledge, which included study in Egyptology and navigation on land or sea.

This Fingerprint Classic, *The Mystery at Number 31, New Inn,* was first published in 1912. It features keen observation and careful reasoning that mystery lovers will enjoy.

TABLE OF CONTENTS

CHAPTER 1
THE MYSTERIOUS PATIENT

As I look back over the years of my association with John Thorndyke, I am able to recall a wealth of adventures and strange experiences such as falls to the lot of very few men who pass their lives within hearing of Big Ben. Many of these experiences I have already placed on record, but it now occurs to me that I have hitherto left unrecorded one that is, perhaps, the most astonishing and incredible of the whole series. It was an adventure that has for me the added interest that it inaugurated my permanent association with my learned and talented friend and marked the close of a rather unhappy and unprofitable period of my life.

Memory, retracing the journey through the passing years to the starting point of those strange events, lands me in a shabby little ground floor room in a house near the Walworth end of Lower Kennington Lane. A couple of framed diplomas on the wall, a card of Snellen's vision test, and a stethoscope lying on the writing table proclaim it to be a doctor's examination room. My own position in the round-backed chair at this table proclaims me the practitioner in charge.

It was nearly nine o'clock. The noisy little clock on the mantelpiece announced the fact and by its frantic ticking seemed as anxious as I to get the office hours over. Another minute and I could turn down the gas and shut the outer door. The fussy little clock gave a sort of preliminary cough, as if it should say, "Ahem, ladies and gentlemen, I am about to strike," and at that moment, the apothecary's assistant opened the door. Thrusting in his head, he uttered one word. "Gentleman."

Extreme economy of words is apt to result in ambiguity, but I understood. In Kennington Lane, the race of mere men and women appeared to be extinct. They were all gentlemen—unless they were ladies or children. The present nobleman appeared to favor the aristocratic recreation of driving a carriage. As he entered the room, he touched his hat, closed the door somewhat carefully, and then without remark handed me a note that bore the superscription "Dr. Stillbury."

"You understand," I said, as I prepared to open the envelope, "that I am not Dr. Stillbury. He is away at present, and I am looking after his patients."

"It doesn't matter," the man replied. "You'll do as well."

At this I opened the envelope and read the note, which was quite brief and at first sight in no way remarkable.

"Dear Sir," it ran. "Would you kindly come and see a friend of mine who is staying with me? The bearer of this will give you further particulars and convey you to the house. Yours truly, H. Weiss."

There was no address on the paper and no date, and the writer was unknown to me.

"This note," I said, "refers to some further particulars. What are they?"

The messenger passed his hand over his hair with a ges-
ture of embarrassment. "It's a ridiculous affair," he said with a
contemptuous laugh. "If I had been Mr. Weiss, I wouldn't have
had nothing to do with it. The sick gentleman, Mr. Graves, is
one of them people what can't bear doctors. He's been ailing
now for a week or two, but nothing would induce him to see
a doctor. Mr. Weiss did everything he could to persuade him,
but it was no-go. He wouldn't. However, it seems Weiss threat-
ened to send for a medical man on his own account because,
you see, he was getting a bit nervous, and then Mr. Graves
gave way. But only on one condition. He said the doctor was
to come from a distance and was not to be told who he was
or where he lived or anything about him. He made Mr. Weiss
promise to keep to that condition before he'd let him send. So
Mr. Weiss promised, and of course he's got to keep his word."

"But," I said, with a smile, "you've just told me his name—
if his name really is Graves."

"You can form your own opinion on that," said the coachman.

"And," I added, "as to not being told where he lives, I can
see that for myself. I'm not blind, you know."

"We'll take care of what you see," the man replied. "The
question is: will you take on the job?"

Yes, that was the question, and I considered it for some
time before replying. We medical men are pretty familiar
with the kind of person who *can't bear doctors,* and we like to
have as little to do with him as possible. He is a thankless and
unsatisfactory patient. Dealing with him is unpleasant. He
gives a great deal of trouble and responds badly to treatment. If
this had been my own practice, I would have declined the case
immediately. But it was not my practice. I was only a deputy.
I could not lightly refuse work that would yield a profit to my
principal, unpleasant though it might be.

As I turned the matter over in my mind, I unconsciously
scrutinized my visitor—somewhat to his embarrassment—and

I liked his appearance as little as I liked his mission. He kept his station near the door where the light was dim, but I could see that he had a somewhat sly, unattractive face and a greasy red moustache that seemed out of character with his rather ordinary uniform, though this was mere opinion. He wore a wig too—not that there was anything discreditable in that—and the thumbnail of the hand that held his hat bore disfiguring traces of some injury which, again, though unsightly, in no way reflected on his moral character. Lastly, he watched me keenly with a mixture of anxiety and sly complacency that I found distinctly unpleasant. In a general way, he impressed me disagreeably. I did not like the look of him at all, but nevertheless I decided to undertake the case.

"I suppose," I answered at length, "it is no affair of mine who the patient is or where he lives. But how do you propose to manage the business? Am I to be led to the house blindfolded, like the visitor to the bandit's cave?"

The man grinned slightly and looked very decidedly relieved. "No, sir," he answered. "We ain't going to blindfold you. I've got a carriage outside. I don't think you'll see much out of that."

"Very well." I opened the door to let him out. "I'll be with you in a minute. I suppose you can't give me any idea as to what is the matter with the patient?"

"No, sir, I can't," he replied, and he went out to see to the carriage.

I slipped into a bag an assortment of emergency drugs and a few diagnostic instruments, turned down the gas, and passed out through the surgery. The carriage was standing at the curb, guarded by the coachman. It was a large carriage, such as is used by some commercial travelers. The usual glass windows had been replaced by wooden shutters that were intended to conceal the interior space. The doors were capable of being locked from the outside with a key.

As I emerged from the house, the coachman unlocked the door and held it open.

"How long will the journey take?" I asked, pausing with my foot on the step.

The coachman considered a moment or two and replied, "It took me, I should say, nigh upon half an hour to get here."

This was unpleasant to hear. A half an hour each way and a half an hour at the patient's house. At that rate it would be half past ten before I was home again, and then it was quite probable that I would find some other untimely messenger waiting on the doorstep. With a mutter against the unknown Mr. Graves, I stepped into the uninviting vehicle. Instantly the coachman slammed the door and turned the key, leaving me in total darkness.

One comfort was left to me—my pipe was in my pocket. I loaded it in the dark and, having lit it with a wax match, took the opportunity to inspect the interior of my prison. It was a shabby affair. The moth-eaten state of the blue cloth cushions seemed to suggest that it had been long out of regular use; the floor covering was worn into holes; ordinary internal fittings there were none. But the appearances suggested that the crazy vehicle had been prepared with considerable forethought for its present use. The inside handles of the doors had apparently been removed, the wooden shutters were permanently fixed in their places, and a paper label stuck below each window had the suspicious appearance of having been put there to cover the painted name and address of the stable keeper who had originally owned the carriage.

These observations gave me abundant food for reflection. This Mr. Weiss must be an excessively conscientious man if he had considered that his promise to Mr. Graves committed him to such extraordinary precautions. Evidently no mere following of the letter of the law was enough to satisfy his sensitive conscience. Unless he had reasons for sharing Mr. Graves's unreasonable desire for secrecy—for one could not suppose that the patient had taken these measures of concealment himself.

The further suggestions that evolved themselves from this consideration were a little disquieting. Where was I being carried and for what purpose? The idea that I was bound for some den of thieves where I might be robbed and possibly murdered, I dismissed with a smile. Thieves do not make elaborately concerted plans to rob poor devils like me; poverty has its compensations in that respect. But there were other possibilities. Imagination backed by experience had no difficulty in conjuring up a number of situations in which a medical man might be called upon, with or without coercion, either to witness or actively to participate in the commission of some unlawful act.

Reflections of this kind occupied me during this strange journey. And the monotony was relieved, too, by other distractions. I was, for example, greatly interested to notice how, when one sense is in abeyance, the other senses rouse into a compensating intensity of perception. I sat smoking my pipe in darkness which was absolute except for the dim glow from the smoldering tobacco. I seemed to be cut off from all knowledge of the world without, but yet I was not. The vibrations of the carriage with its hard springs and iron-tired wheels registered accurately and plainly the character of the roadway. The harsh rattle of granite stones, the soft bumpiness of asphalt, the smooth rumble of wood pavement, the jarring and swerving of crossed tram-lines—all were easily recognizable and together sketched the general features of the neighborhood through which I was passing. And the sense of hearing filled in the details. Now the hoot of a tugboat's whistle told of proximity to the river. A sudden and brief hollow reverberation announced the passage under a railway arch—which, by the way, happened several times during the journey. When I heard the familiar whistle of a railway guard followed by the quick snorts of a skidding locomotive, I had as clear a picture of a heavy passenger train moving out of a station as if I had seen it in broad daylight.

I had just finished my pipe and knocked out the ashes on the heel of my boot when the carriage slowed down and entered a covered entryway that I could tell by the hollow echoes. Then I distinguished the clang of heavy wooden gates being closed behind me, and a moment or two later the carriage door was unlocked and opened. I stepped out blinking into a covered passage paved with cobbles and apparently leading down to the stables. It was all in darkness, and I had no time to make any detailed observations, as the carriage had drawn up opposite a side door which was open and in which stood a woman holding a lighted candle.

"Is that the doctor?" she asked, speaking with a rather pronounced German accent and shading the candle with her hand as she peered at me.

I answered in the affirmative, and she then exclaimed, "I am glad you have come. Mr. Weiss will be so relieved. Come in, please."

I followed her across a dark passage into a dark room where she set the candle down on a chest of drawers and turned to depart. At the door, however, she paused and looked back.

"It is not a very nice room to ask you into," she said. "We are very untidy just now, but you must excuse us. We have had so much anxiety about poor Mr. Graves."

"He has been ill some time then?"

"Yes. Some little time. At intervals, you know. Sometimes better, sometimes not so well."

As she spoke, she gradually backed out into the passage but did not go away at once. I accordingly pursued my inquiries. "He has not been seen by any doctor, has he?"

"No," she answered, "he has refused to see a doctor. That has been troubling to us. Mr. Weiss has been very anxious about him. He will be so glad to hear that you have come. I had better go and tell him. Perhaps you will kindly sit down until he is able to come to you," and with this she departed on her mission.

It struck me as a little odd that, considering his anxiety and the apparent urgency of the case, Mr. Weiss should not have been waiting to receive me. And when several minutes elapsed without his appearing, the oddness of the circumstance impressed me still more. Having no desire after the journey in the carriage to sit down, I whiled away the time by an inspection of the room. And a very curious room it was—bare, dirty, neglected, and apparently, unused. A faded carpet had been flung untidily on the floor. A small, shabby table stood in the middle of the room, and beyond this, three upholstered chairs and a chest of drawers formed the entire set of furniture. No pictures hung on the moldy walls, no curtains covered the shuttered windows, and the dark drapery of cobwebs that hung from the ceiling hinted at months of neglect and disuse.

The chest of drawers—an incongruous article of furniture for what seemed to be a dining room—as being the nearest and best lighted object received most of my attention. It was a fine old chest of nearly black mahogany, very battered and in the last stages of decay, but originally a piece of some value. Regretful of its fallen estate, I looked it over with some interest and had just observed on its lower corner a little label bearing the printed inscription "Lot 201" when I heard footsteps descending the stairs. A moment later the door opened and a shadowy figure appeared standing close by the threshold.

"Good evening, Doctor," said the stranger in a deep, quiet voice and with a distinct, though not strong, German accent. "I must apologize for keeping you waiting."

I acknowledged the apology somewhat stiffly and asked, "You are Mr. Weiss, I presume?"

"Yes. It is very good of you to come so far and so late at night and to make no objection to the absurd conditions that my poor friend has imposed."

"Not at all," I replied. "It is my business to go when and where I am wanted, and it is not my business to inquire into the private affairs of my patients."

"That is very true, sir," he agreed cordially, "and I am much obliged to you for taking that very proper view of the case. I pointed that out to my friend, but he is not a very reasonable man. He is very secretive and rather suspicious by nature."

"So I inferred. And as to his condition, is he seriously ill?"

"Ah," said Mr. Weiss, "that is what I want you to tell me. I am very much puzzled about him."

"But what is the nature of his illness? What does he complain of?"

"He makes very few complaints of any kind although he is obviously ill. But the fact is that he is hardly ever more than half-awake. He lies in a kind of dreamy stupor from morning to night."

This struck me as excessively strange and by no means in agreement with the patient's energetic refusal to see a doctor.

"Does he never rouse completely?"

"Oh, yes," Mr. Weiss answered quickly. "He rouses from time to time and is then quite rational and, as you may have gathered, rather obstinate. That is the peculiar and puzzling feature in the case, this alternation between a state of stupor and an almost normal and healthy condition. But perhaps you had better see him and judge for yourself. He had a rather severe attack just now. Follow me, please. The stairs are rather dark."

The stairs were very dark, and I noticed that they were without any covering of carpet, so that our footsteps resounded dismally as if we were in an empty house. I stumbled up after my guide, feeling my way by the handrail. On the first floor I followed him into a room similar in size to the one below and very barely furnished, though less squalid than the other. A single candle at the far end threw its feeble light on a figure in the bed, leaving the rest of the room in a dim twilight.

As Mr. Weiss tiptoed into the chamber, a woman—the one who had spoken to me below—rose from a chair by the bedside and quietly left the room by a second door. My guide halted and, looking fixedly at the figure in the bed, called out, "Philip! Philip! Here is the doctor come to see you."

He paused for a moment or two and, receiving no answer, said, "He seems to be dozing as usual. Will you go and see what you can make of him?"

I stepped forward to the bedside, leaving Mr. Weiss at the end of the room near the door by which we had entered, where he remained, slowly and noiselessly pacing in the dimness. By the light of the candle I saw an elderly man with good features and a refined, intelligent, and even attractive face, but dreadfully emaciated, bloodless, and sallow. He lay quite motionless except for the scarcely perceptible rise and fall of his chest. His eyes were nearly closed, his features relaxed, and though he was not actually asleep, he seemed to be in a dreamy, lethargic state, as if under the influence of some narcotic.

I watched him for a minute or so, timing his slow breathing by my watch, and then suddenly and sharply I addressed him by name, but the only response was a slight lifting of the eyelids, which after a brief drowsy glance at me slowly subsided to their former position.

I proceeded to make a physical examination. First I felt his pulse, grasping his wrist with intentional brusqueness in the hope of rousing him from his stupor. The beats were slow, feeble, and slightly irregular, giving clear evidence, if any was needed, of his generally lowered vitality. I listened carefully to his heart, the sounds of which were very distinct through the thin walls of his emaciated chest, but I found nothing abnormal beyond the feebleness and uncertainty of its action. Then I turned my attention to his eyes, which I examined closely with the aid of the candle and my ophthalmoscopic lens, raising the lid somewhat roughly so as to expose the whole of the iris. He submitted without resistance to my rather rough handling of these sensitive structures and showed no signs of discomfort even when I brought the candle flame to within a couple of inches of his eyes.

But this extraordinary tolerance of light was easily explained by closer examination, for the pupils were contracted to such an extreme degree that only the very minutest point of black was visible at the center of the gray iris. Nor was this the only abnormal peculiarity of the sick man's eyes. As he lay on his back, the right iris sagged down slightly towards its center, showing a distinctly concave surface, and when I contrived to produce a slight but quick movement of the eyeball, a perceptible undulatory movement could be detected. The patient had what is known as a tremulous iris, a condition that is seen in cases where the lens has been extracted for the cure of cataract, or where it has become accidentally displaced, leaving the iris unsupported. In the present case, the complete condition of the iris made it clear that no operation had been performed. The inference was that the patient had suffered from the accident known as "dislocation of the lens." This led to the further inference that he was almost completely blind in the right eye.

This conclusion was indeed to some extent contradicted by a deep indentation on the bridge of the nose, evidently produced by spectacles, and by marks that I looked for and found behind the ears. As to the nature of the patient's illness, only one opinion seemed possible. It was a clear and typical case of opium or morphine poisoning. All his symptoms seemed to point to this conclusion with absolute certainty: the coated tongue, which he protruded slowly and tremulously in response to a command bawled in his ear; his yellow skin and ghastly expression; his contracted pupils and the stupor, from which he could hardly be roused by the roughest handling and which yet did not amount to actual insensibility. All these formed a distinct and coherent group of symptoms, not only pointing plainly to the nature of the drug, but also suggesting a very formidable dose.

But this conclusion in its turn raised a very awkward and difficult question. If a large—a poisonous—dose of the drug had been taken, how, and by whom had that dose been administered? The closest scrutiny of the patient's arms and legs failed to reveal a single mark such as would be made by a hypodermic needle. This man was clearly no common drug addict; and in the absence of the usual sprinkling of needle marks, there was nothing to suggest whether the drug had been taken voluntarily by the patient himself or administered by someone else.

And then there remained the possibility that I might be mistaken in my diagnosis. I felt pretty confident, but the wise man always holds a doubt in reserve. And in the present case with regard to the obviously serious condition of the patient, such a doubt was very disturbing. Indeed, as I pocketed my stethoscope and took a last look at the motionless, silent figure, I realized that my position was one of extraordinary difficulty and perplexity. On the one hand my suspicions—aroused, naturally enough, by the very unusual circumstances that surrounded my visit—inclined me to extreme reticence, while on the other it was evidently my duty to give any information that might prove beneficial to the patient.

As I turned away from the bed, Mr. Weiss stopped his slow pacing and faced me. The feeble light of the candle now fell on him, and I saw him distinctly for the first time. He did not impress me favorably. He was a heavyset, round-shouldered man, a typical fair German with tow-colored hair, greased and brushed down smoothly, a large, ragged, sandy beard, and coarse, sketchy features. His nose was large and thick with a bulbous end and inclined to a reddish purple, a tint that extended to the adjacent parts of his face as if the color had run. His eyebrows were large and beetling, overhanging deep-set eyes, and he wore a pair of spectacles that gave him a somewhat owlish expression. His exterior was unattractive, and I was in a state of mind that rendered me easily receptive of an unfavorable impression.

The Mysterious Patient

"Well," he said, "what do you make of him?"

I hesitated, still perplexed by the conflicting necessities of caution and frankness, but at length replied, "I think rather badly of him, Mr. Weiss. He is in a very low state."

"Yes, I can see that. But have you come to any decision as to the nature of his illness?"

There was a tone of anxiety and suppressed eagerness in the question which, while it was natural enough in the circumstances, by no means allayed my suspicions, but rather influenced me on the side of caution.

"I cannot give a very definite opinion at present," I replied guardedly. "The symptoms are rather obscure and might very well indicate several different conditions. They might be due to congestion of the brain, and if no other explanation were possible, I should incline to that view. The alternative is some narcotic poison, such as opium or morphine."

"But that is quite impossible. There is no such drug in the house, and as he never leaves his room now, he could not get any from outside."

"What about the servants?" I asked.

"There are no servants except for my housekeeper, and she is absolutely trustworthy."

"Might he have some store of the drug that you are not aware of? Is he left alone much?"

"Very seldom indeed. I spend as much time with him as I can, and when I am not able to be in the room, Mrs. Schallibaum, my housekeeper, sits with him."

"Is he often as drowsy as he is now?"

"Oh, very often; in fact, I should say that is his usual condition. He rouses up now and again, and then he is quite lucid and natural for perhaps an hour or so. But presently he becomes drowsy again and dozes off and remains asleep for hours on end. Do you know of any disease that takes people in that way?"

"No," I answered. "The symptoms are not exactly like those of any disease that is known to me. But they are very much like those of opium poisoning."

"But, my dear sir," Mr. Weiss spoke impatiently, "since it is clearly impossible that it can be opium poisoning, it must be something else. Now what else can it be? You were speaking of congestion of the brain."

"Yes. But the problem with that is the very complete recovery that seems to take place in the intervals."

. "I would not say very complete," said Mr. Weiss. "The recovery is rather comparative. He is lucid and fairly natural in his manner, but he is still dull and lethargic. He does not, for instance, show any desire to go out, or even to leave his room."

I pondered these rather contradictory statements. Clearly Mr. Weiss did not want to entertain the theory of opium poisoning, which was natural enough if he had no knowledge of the drug having been used. But still—

"I suppose," said Mr. Weiss, "you have had no experience of sleeping sickness?"

The suggestion startled me. I had not. Very few people had. At that time practically nothing was known about the disease. It was a mere pathological curiosity, almost unheard of except by a few doctors in remote parts of Africa. It was hardly referred to in the textbooks. To me, its symptoms were absolutely unknown.

"No, I have not," I replied. "The disease is nothing more than a name to me. But why do you ask? Has Mr. Graves been abroad?"

"Yes. He has been traveling for the last three or four years, and I know that he spent some time recently in West Africa, where this disease occurs. In fact, it was from him that I first heard about it."

This was a new fact, and it shook my confidence in my diagnosis considerably and inclined me to reconsider my suspicions. If Mr. Weiss was lying to me, he now had me at a decided disadvantage.

"What do you think?" he asked. "Is it possible that this can be sleeping sickness?"

"I should not like to say that it is impossible," I replied. "The disease is practically unknown to me. I have never practiced out of England and have had no occasion to study it. Until I have looked the subject up, I should not be in a position to give an opinion. Of course, if I could see Mr. Graves in one of what we may call his *lucid intervals,* I should be able to form a better idea. Do you think that could be managed?"

"It might. I see the importance of it and will certainly do my best, but he is a difficult man, a very difficult man. I sincerely hope it is not sleeping sickness."

"Why?"

"Because—as I understood from him—that disease is invariably fatal. There seems to be no cure. Do you think you will be able to decide when you see him again?"

"I hope so," I replied. "I shall look up the authorities and see exactly what the symptoms are—that is, so far as they are known."

"And in the meantime?"

"We will give him some medicine and attend to his general condition, and you had better let me see him again as soon as possible." I was about to say that the effect of the medicine itself might throw some light on the patient's condition, but as I proposed to treat him for morphine poisoning, I thought it wiser to keep this item of information to myself. Accordingly, I confined myself to a few general directions as to the care of the patient, to which Mr. Weiss listened attentively. "And," I concluded, "we must not lose sight of the drug question. You had better search the room carefully and keep a close watch on the patient, especially during his intervals of wakefulness."

"Very well, doctor," Mr. Weiss replied. "I will do all that you tell me, and I will send for you again as soon as possible, if you do not object to poor Graves's ridiculous conditions. And now, if you will allow me to pay your fee, I will go and order the carriage, while you are writing the prescription."

"There is no need for a prescription," I said. "I will make up some medicine and give it to the coachman."

Mr. Weiss seemed inclined to object to this arrangement, but I had my own reasons for insisting on it. Modern prescriptions are not difficult to read, and I did not wish Mr. Weiss to know what treatment the patient was having.

As soon as I was left alone, I returned to the bedside and once more looked down at the impassive figure. And as I looked, my suspicions revived. It was very like morphine poisoning; and if it was morphine, it was no common, medicinal dose that had been given. I opened my bag and took out my hypodermic case from which I extracted a little tube of atropine tablets. Shaking out into my hand a couple of the tiny discs, I drew down the patient's lip and slipped the little tablets under his tongue. Then I quickly replaced the tube and dropped the case into my bag. I had hardly done so when the door opened softly, and the housekeeper entered the room.

"How do you find Mr. Graves?" she asked in what I thought a very unnecessarily low tone, considering the patient's lethargic state.

"He seems to be very ill," I answered.

"I am sorry to hear that. We have been anxious about him."

She seated herself on the chair by the bedside, and shading the candle from the patient's face and her own too, produced from a bag that hung from her waist a half-finished stocking and began to knit silently with the skill characteristic of the German housewife. I looked at her attentively, though she was so much in the shadow that I could see her but indistinctly. Yet she was not an unattractive woman. She had the air of a person of good social position; her features were good enough, and her coloring, although a little unusual, was not unpleasant. Like Mr. Weiss, she had very fair hair, greased, parted in the middle and brushed down as smoothly as the painted hair of a Dutch doll. She appeared to have no eyebrows at all owing no doubt to the light color of the hair. The doll-like character was emphasized by her eyes, which were either brown or dark gray. I could not see which. A further peculiarity consisted in a "habit spasm," such as one often sees in nervous children; a periodic quick jerk of the head, as if a dangling lock of hair was being shaken off the cheek. Her age I judged to be about thirty-five.

The carriage, which one might have expected to be waiting, seemed to take some time in getting ready. I sat with growing impatience, listening to the sick man's soft breathing and the click of the housekeeper's knitting needles. I wanted to get home, not only for my own sake, as the patient's condition made it highly desirable that the remedies should be given as quickly as possible. But the minutes dragged on, and I was on the point of questioning, when a bell rang on the landing.

"The carriage is ready," said Mrs. Schallibaum. "Let me light you down the stairs."

She rose and taking the candle preceded me to the head of the stairs where she stood holding the light over the rail as I descended and crossed the passage to the open side door. The carriage was drawn up in the covered way as I could see by the faint glimmer of the distant candle, which also enabled me dimly to discern the coachman standing close by in the shadow. I looked round, rather expecting to see Mr. Weiss, but as he made no appearance, I entered the carriage. The door was immediately closed and locked, and I then heard the heavy bolts of the gates withdrawn and the loud creaking of hinges. The carriage moved out slowly and stopped; the gates slammed shut behind me; I felt the lurch as the coachman climbed to his seat, and we started forward.

My reflections during the return journey were the reverse of agreeable. I could not rid myself of the conviction that I was being involved in some very suspicious proceedings. It was possible of course, that this feeling was due to the strange secrecy that surrounded my connection with this case, that had I made my visit under ordinary conditions I might have found in the patient's symptoms nothing to excite suspicion or alarm. It might be so, but that consideration did not comfort me.

Then, my diagnosis might be wrong. It might be that this was, in reality, a case of some brain affliction accompanied by compression, such as slow hemorrhage, abscess, tumor, or simple congestion. These cases were very difficult at times. But the appearances in this one did not consistently agree with the symptoms accompanying any of these conditions. As to sleeping sickness, it was perhaps a more hopeful suggestion, but I could not decide for or against it until I had more knowledge. Against this view was the weighty fact that the symptoms did agree exactly with the theory of morphine poisoning.

But even so, there was no conclusive evidence of any criminal act. The patient might be a confirmed drug addict and the symptoms heightened by deliberate deception. The cunning of these unfortunates is proverbial and is only equaled by their secretiveness and deception. It would be quite possible for this man to feign profound stupor so long as he was watched, and then, when left alone for a few minutes, to nip out of bed and help himself from some secret store of the drug. This would be quite in character with his objection to seeing a doctor and his desire for secrecy. But still, I did not believe it to be the true explanation. In spite of all the various alternative possibilities, my suspicions came back to Mr. Weiss and the strange, taciturn woman, and refused to budge.

All of the circumstances of the case were suspicious: the elaborate preparations implied by the state of the carriage in which I was traveling; the makeshift appearance of the house; the absence of ordinary domestic servants although a coachman was kept; the evident desire of Mr. Weiss and the woman to avoid thorough inspection of their persons; and, above all, the fact that the former had told me a deliberate lie. For he had lied beyond all doubt. His statement as to the almost continuous stupor was absolutely irreconcilable with his other statement as to the patient's willfulness and obstinacy and even more irreconcilable with the deep and comparatively fresh marks of the spectacles on the patient's nose. That man had certainly worn spectacles within twenty-four hours, which he would hardly have done if he had been in a state bordering on coma.

The stopping of the carriage interrupted my reflections. The door was unlocked and thrown open, and I emerged from my dark and stuffy prison opposite my own house.

"I will let you have the medicine in a minute or two," I said to the coachman. As I let myself in with my key, my mind came back swiftly from the general circumstances of the case to the very critical condition of the patient. Already I was regretting that I had not taken more energetic measures to rouse him and restore his flagging vitality, for it would be a terrible thing if he should take a turn for the worse and die before the coachman returned with the remedies. Spurred on by this alarming thought, I made up the medicines quickly and carried the hastily wrapped bottles out to the man, whom I found standing by the horse's head.

"Get back as quickly as you can," I said, "and tell Mr. Weiss to lose no time in giving the patient the dose in the small bottle. The directions are on the labels."

The coachman took the packages from me without reply, climbed to his seat, touched the horse with his whip, and drove off at a rapid pace towards Newington Butts.

The little clock in the consulting room showed that it was close to eleven; time for a tired doctor to be thinking of bed. But I was not sleepy.

Over my frugal supper I found myself taking up anew the thread of my meditations. Afterwards, I looked in Stillbury's reference library for information on the subject of sleeping sickness, but learned no more than that it was "a rare and obscure disease of which very little was known at present." I read about morphine poisoning and was only further confirmed in the belief that my diagnosis was correct, which would have been more satisfactory if the circumstances had been different.

My interest in the case was not merely academic; I was in a position of great difficulty and responsibility and had to decide on a course of action. Should I maintain the professional secrecy to which I was tacitly committed, or ought I to convey a hint to the police?

Suddenly, and with a singular feeling of relief, I thought of my old friend and fellow student, John Thorndyke, now a leading authority on medical jurisprudence. I had been associated with him temporarily in one case as his assistant, and had then been deeply impressed by his versatile learning, his acuteness, and his marvelous resourcefulness. Thorndyke was a lawyer in extensive practice, and so he would be able to tell me at once what was my duty from a legal point of view. And, as he was also a doctor of medicine, he would understand the requirements of medical practice. If I could find time to call at the Temple and lay the case before him, all my difficulties would be resolved.

Anxiously I opened my visiting list to see what kind of day's work was in store for me on the morrow. It was not a heavy day, even allowing for one or two extra calls in the morning; even so, I was doubtful whether it would allow my going so far from my district, until my eye caught the name of Burton. Mr. Burton lived in one of the old houses on the east side of Bouverie Street, less than five minutes walk from Thorndyke's chambers in King's Bench Walk; and he was, moreover, a "chronic" who could safely be left for the last. When I was done with Mr. Burton, I could look in on my friend. I could allow myself time for quite a long chat with him, and by taking a cab, still get back in good time for the evening's work.

This was a great comfort. Having entered the engagement in my visiting list, I rose in greatly improved spirits just as the little clock impatiently chimed the hour of midnight.

CHAPTER 2
THORNDYKE DEVISES A SCHEME

As I entered the Temple by the Tudor Street gate, the look of the place smote my senses with an air of agreeable familiarity. I had spent many a delightful hour here when working with Thorndyke on the remarkable Hornby case, which the newspapers had called "The Case of the Red Thumb Mark." The place was thus endeared to me.

My brisk tattoo on the little brass knocker brought to the door no one less than Thorndyke himself, and the warmth of his greeting made me at once proud and ashamed. For I had not only been an absentee, I had been a very poor correspondent.

"The prodigal has returned, Polton," he exclaimed, looking into the room. "Here is Dr. Jervis."

I followed him into the room and found Polton—his confidential servant, laboratory assistant, and skilled craftsman—setting out the tea tray on a small table. The little man shook hands cordially with me, and his face crinkled up into the sort of smile that one might expect to see on a benevolent walnut.

"We've often talked about you, sir," said he. "The doctor was wondering only yesterday when you were coming back to us."

As I was not "coming back to them" quite in the sense intended, I felt a little guilty but reserved my confidences for Thorndyke's ear and replied in polite generalities. Then Polton fetched the teapot from the laboratory, made up the fire, and departed. Thorndyke and I subsided, as of old, into our respective armchairs.

"And whence do you spring from in this unexpected fashion?" my colleague asked. "You look as if you had been making professional visits."

"I have. The base of operations is in Lower Kennington Lane."

"Ah! Then you are 'back once more on the old trail'?"

"Yes," I answered with a laugh. " 'The old trail, the long trail, the trail that is always new.' "

"And leads nowhere," Thorndyke added grimly.

I laughed again, not very heartily, for there was an uncomfortable element of truth in my friend's remark to which my own experience bore only too complete testimony. The medical practitioner whose lack of means forces him to subsist by taking temporary charge of other men's practices is apt to find that the passing years bring him little but gray hairs and a wealth of disagreeable experience.

"You will have to drop it, Jervis. You will indeed," Thorndyke resumed after a pause. "This casual employment is preposterous for a man of your class and professional attainments. Have you forgotten my proposal?"

"I should be an ungrateful brute if I had."

"Very well. I repeat it now. Come to me as my junior. Read for the bar and work with me. With your abilities, you will have a chance of something like a career. I want you, Jervis," he added earnestly. "I must have an assistant with my increasing practice, and you are the one I want. We are old and tried friends; we have worked together; we like and trust one another, and you are the best man for the job that I know. Come; I am not going to take a refusal. This is an ultimatum."

"And what is the alternative?" I asked with a smile at his eagerness.

"There isn't any. You are going to say yes."

"I believe I am," I answered not without emotion. "I am more pleased with your offer and more grateful than I can tell you. But we must leave the final arrangements for our next meeting—in a week or so, I hope—for I have to be back in an hour, and I want to consult you on a matter of some importance."

"Very well," said Thorndyke. "We will leave the formal agreement for consideration at our next meeting. What is it that you want my opinion on?"

"The fact is," I said, "I am in a rather awkward dilemma, and I want you to tell me what you think I ought to do."

Thorndyke paused in the act of refilling my cup and glanced at me with unmistakable anxiety. "Nothing of an unpleasant nature, I hope," said he.

"No, no; nothing of the kind," I answered with a smile. "It is nothing that concerns me personally at all," I continued. "It is a question of professional responsibility. But I had better give you an account of the affair in a complete narrative, as I know that you like to have your data in a regular and consecutive order."

Thereupon I proceeded to relate the history of my visit to the mysterious Mr. Graves, not omitting any single circumstance or detail that I could recollect.

Thorndyke listened from the very beginning of my story with the closest attention. His face was the most impassive that I have ever seen. It was ordinarily as inscrutable as a bronze mask, but to me, who knew him intimately, there was a certain something—a change of color, perhaps, or an additional sparkle of the eye—that told me when his curious passion for investigation was piqued. And now, as I told him of that weird journey and the strange, secret house to which it had brought me, I could see that it offered a problem after his very heart. During the whole of my narration, he sat motionless as a statue, evidently committing the whole story to memory, detail by detail. Even when I had finished, he remained for an appreciable time without moving or speaking.

At length he looked up at me. "This is a very extraordinary affair, Jervis," he said.

"Very," I agreed. "And the question that is agitating me is: what is to be done?"

He said meditatively, "That is the question and an uncommonly difficult question it is. It really involves settling the antecedent question first: what is it that is happening at that house? We must go slowly, Jervis," he replied. "We must carefully separate the legal issues from the medical and avoid confusing what we know with what we suspect. Now with reference to the medical aspects of the case: the first question that confronts us is that of sleeping sickness, and here we are in a difficulty. We have not enough knowledge. Neither of us, I take it, has ever seen a case, and the descriptions are inadequate. From what I know of the disease, its symptoms agree with those in your case with respect to the gradually increasing periods of lethargy alternating with periods of apparent recovery. A more important fact is that, as far as I know, extreme contraction of the pupils is not a symptom of sleeping sickness. To sum up, the probabilities are against sleeping sickness, but with our insufficient knowledge, we cannot definitely exclude it."

"You think that it may really be sleeping sickness?"

"No; personally I do not entertain that theory for a moment. But I am considering the evidence apart from our opinions on the subject. We have to accept it as a conceivable hypothesis that it may be sleeping sickness because we cannot positively prove that it is not. That is all. But when we come to the hypothesis of morphine poisoning, the case is different. The symptoms agree with those of morphine poisoning in every respect. There is no exception or disagreement whatever. The common sense of the matter is therefore that we adopt morphine poisoning as our working diagnosis, which is what you seem to have done."

"Yes. For purposes of treatment."

"Exactly. For medical purposes you adopted the more probable view and dismissed the less probable. That was the reasonable thing to do. But for legal purposes you must entertain both possibilities; for the hypothesis of poisoning involves serious legal issues, whereas the hypothesis of disease involves no legal issues at all."

"That doesn't sound very helpful," I remarked.

"It indicates the necessity for caution," he retorted.

"Yes, I see that. But what is your own opinion of the case?"

"Well," he said, "let us consider the facts in order. Here is a man who we assume is under the influence of a poisonous dose of morphine. The question is, did he take that dose himself or was it administered to him by some other person? If he took it himself, with what object did he take it? The history that was given to you seems to exclude the idea of addiction. Your man does not reduce himself to a state of coma. He usually keeps well within the limits of the tolerance that has been established. The conclusion that emerges is, I think, that the drug was administered by some other person; and the most likely person seems to be Mr. Weiss."

"Isn't morphine a very unusual poison?"

"Very; and most inconvenient except in a single, fatal dose, by reason of the rapidity with which tolerance of the drug is established. But we must not forget that slow morphine poisoning might be eminently suitable in certain cases. The manner in which it enfeebles the will, confuses the judgment, and debilitates the body might make it very useful to a poisoner whose aim was to get some instrument or document executed, such as a will, deed, or assignment. And death could be produced afterwards by other means. You see the important bearing of this?"

"You mean in respect of a death certificate?"

"Yes. Suppose Mr. Weiss was to have given a large dose of morphine. He then sends for you and throws out a suggestion of sleeping sickness. If you accept the suggestion, he is pretty safe. He can repeat the process until he kills his victim and then get a certificate from you that will cover the murder. It was quite an ingenious scheme. Which, by the way, is characteristic of intricate crimes; your subtle criminal often plans his crime like a genius, but he generally executes it like a fool—as this man seems to have done, if I am not doing him an injustice."

"How has he acted like a fool?"

"In several respects. In the first place, he should have chosen his doctor. A good, brisk, confident man who knows his own mind is the sort of person who would have suited him; a man who would have jumped at a diagnosis and stuck to it; or else an ignorant weakling. It was shockingly unfortunate to run against a cautious scientific practitioner like you, my learned friend. Then, of course, all this secrecy was sheer tomfoolery, exactly calculated to put a careful man on his guard, as it has actually done. If Mr. Weiss is really a criminal, he has mismanaged his affairs badly."

"And you apparently think that he is a criminal?"

"I suspect him deeply. But I should like to ask you one or two questions about him. You say he spoke with a German accent. What command of English had he? Was his vocabulary good? Did he use any German idioms?"

"No. I would say that his English was perfect, and I noticed that his phrases were quite well chosen even for an Englishman."

"Did he seem to you *made-up* in any way; disguised, I mean?"

"I couldn't say. The light was so very feeble."

"You couldn't see the color of his eyes, for instance?"

"No. I think they were gray, but I couldn't be sure."

"And as to the coachman. He wore a wig, you said. Could you see the color of his eyes? Or any peculiarity by which you could recognize him?"

"He had a malformed thumbnail on his right hand. That is all I can say about him."

"He didn't strike you as resembling Weiss in any way—in voice or features?"

"Not at all; and he spoke, as I told you, with a distinct Scotch accent."

"The reason I ask is that if Weiss is attempting to poison this man, the coachman is almost certain to be a confederate and might be a relative. You had better examine him closely if you get another chance."

"I will. And that brings me back to the question, what am I to do? Ought I to report the case to the police?

"I am inclined to think not. You have hardly enough facts. Of course, if Mr. Weiss has administered poison unlawfully and maliciously, he has committed a felony. But you don't know that he administered the poison—if poison has really been administered—and you cannot give any reliable name or any address whatever. Then there is the question of sleeping sickness. You reject it for medical purposes, but you could not swear in a court of law that this is not a case of sleeping sickness."

"No," I admitted, "I could not."

"Then I think the police would decline to move in the matter, and you might find that you had raised a scandal in Dr. Stillbury's practice to no purpose."

"So you think I had better do nothing in the matter?"

"For the present. It is, of course, a medical man's duty to assist justice in any way that is possible. But a doctor is not a detective, and he should not go out of his way to assume police functions. He should keep his eyes and ears open; and though it is not his business to initiate criminal inquiries, it is emphatically his business to be ready, if called upon, to assist justice with information that his special knowledge and opportunities have rendered accessible to him. You see the bearing of this?"

"You mean that I should record what I have seen and heard and say nothing about it until I am asked."

"Yes; if nothing further happens. But if you should be sent for again, I think it is your duty to make further observations with a view, if necessary, to informing the police. It may be, for instance, of vital importance to identify the house, and it is your duty to secure the means of doing so."

"But my dear Thorndyke," I protested, "I have told you how I was conveyed to the house. Now will you kindly explain to me how a man, boxed up in a pitch dark carriage, is going to identify any place to which he may be carried?"

"The problem doesn't appear to me to present any serious difficulties," he replied.

"Doesn't it?" said I. "To me it looks like a pretty solid impossibility. But what do you suggest? Should I break out of the house and run away up the street? Or should I bore a hole through the shutter of the carriage and peep out?"

Thorndyke smiled indulgently. "The methods proposed by my learned friend display a certain crudity inappropriate to the character of a man of science, to say nothing of the disadvantage of letting the enemy into our counsels. No, no, Jervis.

We can do something better than that. Just excuse me for a minute while I run up to the laboratory."

He hurried away to Polton's sanctum on the upper floor, leaving me to speculate on the method by which he proposed that a man should be enabled to see through the wooden shutters of a closed carriage.

"Now," he said, when he returned a couple of minutes later with a small notebook in his hand, "I have set Polton to work on a little appliance that will, I think, solve our difficulty. I will show you how I propose that you should make your observations. First of all, we have to rule the pages of this book into columns."

He sat down at the table and began methodically to divide the pages each into three columns, two quite narrow and one broad. The process occupied some time, during which I sat and watched with impatient curiosity the unhurried, precise movements of Thorndyke's pencil, all agog to hear the promised explanation. He was just finishing the last page when there came a gentle tap at the door, and Polton entered with a satisfied smile on his dry, shrewd-looking face and a small board in his hand.

"Will this do, sir?" he asked.

As he spoke he handed the little board to Thorndyke, who looked at it and passed it to me.

"The very thing, Polton," my friend replied. "Where did you find it? It's of no use for you to pretend that you've made it in about two minutes and a half."

Polton smiled one of his queer, crinkly smiles, and remarking that "it didn't take much making," departed much gratified by the compliment.

"What a wonderful old fellow that man is," Thorndyke observed as Polton retired. "He took in the idea instantly and seems to have produced the finished article by magic at a moment's notice. I suppose you see what your modus operandi is to be?"

I had gathered a clue from the little appliance—a plate of wood about seven inches by five. To one corner of it a pocket compass had been affixed, but it was not quite clear as to the details of the method.

"You can read a compass pretty quickly, I think?" Thorndyke said.

"Of course I can."

"To be sure. And now as to your method of locating this house: here is a pocket reading lamp that you can hook onto the carriage lining. This notebook can be fixed to the board with a rubber band—thus. You observe that the thoughtful Polton has stuck a piece of thread on the glass of the compass to serve as a lubber's line. As soon as you are locked in the carriage, light your lamp. Better have a book with you in case the light is noticed. Take out your watch and put the board on your knee, keeping its long side exactly in a line with the axis of the carriage. Then enter in one narrow column of your notebook the time, in the other the direction shown by the compass, and in the broad column any particulars, including the number of steps the horse makes in a minute. Like this."

He took a loose sheet of paper and made one or two sample entries on it in pencil.

9:40	S.E.	Start from home.
9:41	S.W.	Granite stones.
9:43	S.W.	Wood pavement. Hoofs-104.
9:47	W. by S.	Granite crossing. Asphalt.

"And so on. Note every change of direction with the time. Whenever you hear or feel anything from outside, note it with the time and direction. And don't forget to note any variations in the horse's pace. You follow the process?"

"Perfectly. But do you think the method is accurate enough to fix the position of a house? Remember, this is only a pocket compass with no dial, and it will jump frightfully. And the mode of estimating distance is very rough."

"That is all perfectly true," Thorndyke answered. "But you are overlooking certain important facts. The track chart that you will produce can be checked by other data. The house, for instance, has a covered way by which you could identify it if you knew approximately where to look for it. Then you must remember that your carriage is not traveling over a featureless plain. It is passing through streets, which have a known position and direction and, which can be accurately represented on a map. I think, Jervis, that despite the apparent roughness of the method, if you make your observations carefully, we shall have no trouble in narrowing down the inquiry to a quite small area. If we get the chance, that is to say."

"Yes, if we do. I am doubtful whether Mr. Weiss will require my services again, but I sincerely hope he will. It would be rare sport to locate a secret burrow all unsuspected. But now I must really be off."

"Goodbye then," said Thorndyke, slipping a well-sharpened pencil through the rubber band that fixed the notebook to the board. "Let me know how the adventure progresses—if it progresses at all—and remember, I hold your promise to come and see me again quite soon in any case."

He handed me the board and the lamp, and when I had slipped them into my pocket, we shook hands and I hurried away, a little uneasy at having left my office so long.

CHAPTER 3
TAKING NOTES

The attitude of the suspicious man tends to generate in others the kind of conduct that seems to justify his suspicions. In most of us there lurks a certain strain of mischief which trustfulness disarms but distrust encourages. The inexperienced kitten which approaches us confidingly with arched back and upraised tail, soliciting caresses, generally receives the gentle treatment that it expects; whereas the worldly-wise tomcat, who, in response to friendly advances, scampers away and grins at us suspiciously from the fancied security of an adjacent wall, impels us to accelerate his retreat with a well-directed clod.

Now the proceedings of Mr. H. Weiss resembled those of that tomcat. To a responsible professional man his extraordinary precautions were at once an affront and a challenge. Apart from graver considerations, I found myself dwelling with unholy pleasure on the prospect of locating the secret hiding place from which he seemed to grin at me with such complacent defiance. I lost no time and spared no trouble in preparing myself for the adventure. The very hansom which bore me from the Temple to Kennington Lane was utilized for a preliminary test of Thorndyke's little apparatus. During that brief journey I observed closely, noted the feel and sound of the roadway and timed the trotting of the horse. The result was quite encouraging. It is true that the compass needle oscillated wildly to the vibration of the cab, but still its oscillations took place around a definite point which was the average direction, and it was evident to me that the data it furnished were very fairly reliable. I felt very little doubt, after the preliminary trial, as to my being able to produce a moderately intelligible chart if only I should get an opportunity to exercise my skill.

But it looked as if I should not. Mr. Weiss's promise to send for me again soon was not fulfilled. Three days passed, and still he made no sign. I began to fear that I had been too outspoken, that the shuttered carriage had sought some more confiding and easygoing practitioner, and that our elaborate preparations had been made in vain. When the fourth day drew towards a close and still no summons had come, I was disposed reluctantly to write the case off as a lost opportunity.

And at that moment, in the midst of my regrets, the apothecary's assistant thrust an uncomely head in at the door. His voice was coarse, his accent was hideous, and his grammatical construction beneath contempt, but I forgave him all when I gathered the import of his message.

"Mr. Weiss's carriage is waiting, and he says will you come as quickly as you can because he's took very bad tonight."

I sprang from my chair and hastily collected the necessaries for the journey. I put the little board and the lamp in my overcoat pocket; I overhauled the emergency bag and added to its usual contents a bottle of crystallized medicine which I thought I might require. Then I tucked the evening paper under my arm and went out.

The coachman, who was standing at the horse's head as I emerged, touched his hat and came forward to open the door.

"I have fortified myself for the long drive, you see," I remarked, exhibiting the newspaper as I stepped into the carriage.

"But you can't read in the dark," said he.

"No, but I have provided myself with a lamp," I replied, producing it and striking a match.

He watched me as I lit the lamp and hooked it on the back cushion and observed, "I suppose you found it rather a dull ride last time. It's a longish way. They might have fitted the carriage with an inside lamp. But we shall have to make it a quicker passage tonight. Governor says Mr. Graves is uncommon bad."

With this he slammed the door and locked it. I drew the board from my pocket, laid it on my knee, glanced at my watch, and as the coachman climbed to his seat, I made the first entry in the little book.

> 8:58. W. by S. Start from home. Horse 13 hands.

The first move of the carriage on starting was to turn round as if heading for Newington Butts, and the second entry accordingly read:

> 8:58.00. E. by N.

But this direction was not maintained long. Very soon we turned south and then west and then south again. I sat with my eyes riveted on the compass, following with some difficulty its rapid changes. The needle swung to and fro incessantly but always within a definite arc, the center of which was the true direction. But this direction varied from minute to minute in the most astonishing manner. West, south, east, north, the carriage turned, "boxing" the compass until I lost all count of direction. It was an amazing performance. Considering that the man was driving against time on a mission of life-and-death urgency, his carelessness as to direction was astounding. The tortuousness of the route must have made the journey twice as long as it need have been with a little more careful selection. At least so it appeared to me, though, naturally, I was not in a position to offer an authoritative criticism.

As far as I could judge, we followed the same route as before. Once I heard a tug's whistle and knew that we were near the river, and we passed the railway station, apparently at the same time as on the previous occasion, for I heard a passenger train start and assumed that it was the same train. We crossed quite a number of thoroughfares with railway tracks. I had no idea there were so many. And it was a revelation to me to find how numerous the railway arches were in this part of London and how continually the nature of the roadway varied.

It was by no mean a dull journey this time. The incessant changes of direction and variations in the character of the road kept me uncommonly busy. I had hardly time to scribble down one entry before the compass needle would swing around sharply, showing that we had once more turned a corner. I was quite taken by surprise when the carriage slowed down and turned into the covered way. Very hastily I scribbled down the final entry:

> 9:24.   S.E.   In covered way.

Then I closed the book and slipped it and the board into my pocket. I had just opened out the newspaper when the carriage door was unlocked and opened, whereupon I unhooked and blew out the lamp and pocketed that too, reflecting that it might be useful later.

As on the last occasion, Mrs. Schallibaum stood in the open doorway with a lighted candle. But she was a good deal less self-possessed this time. In fact she looked rather wild and terrified. Even by the candlelight I could see that she was very pale, and she seemed unable to keep still. As she gave me the few necessary words of explanation, she fidgeted incessantly and her hands and feet were in constant movement.

"You had better come up with me at once," she said. "Mr. Graves is much worse tonight. We will wait not for Mr. Weiss."

Without waiting for a reply she quickly ascended the stairs, and I followed. The room was in much the same condition as before, but the patient was not. As soon as I entered the room, a soft, rhythmical gurgle from the bed gave me a very clear warning of danger. I stepped forward quickly and looked down at the prostrate figure, and the warning gathered emphasis. The sick man's ghastly face was yet more ghastly; his eyes were more sunken; his skin more livid; and if he did not babble nonsense, it was because he seemed to be beyond even that. He had all the appearance of a dying man. Even so, feeling convinced that the case was one of morphine poisoning, I was far from confident that I should be able to draw him back from the extreme edge of vitality on which he trembled so insecurely.

"He is very ill? He is dying?"

It was Mrs. Schallibaum's voice; very low, but eager and intense. I turned with my finger on the patient's wrist, and looked into the face of the most thoroughly scared woman I have ever seen. She made no attempt now to avoid the light, but looked me squarely in the face, and I noticed that her eyes were brown and had a curious strained expression.

"Yes," I answered, "he is very ill. He is in great danger."

She still stared at me fixedly for some seconds. And then a very odd thing occurred. Suddenly she squinted—squinted horribly, not with the familiar cross-eyed squint which clowns imitate, but with the divergent squint of extreme near sight or unequal vision. The effect was quite startling. One moment both her eyes were looking straight into mine; the next, one of them rolled around until it looked out of the outside corner, leaving the other gazing steadily forward.

She was evidently conscious of the change, for she turned her head away quickly and reddened somewhat. But it was no time for thoughts of personal appearance.

"You can save him, Doctor. You will not let him die. He must not be allowed to die!"

She spoke with as much passion as if he had been the dearest friend that she had in the world, which I suspected was far from being the case. But her manifest terror had its uses.

"If anything is to be done to save him," I said, "it must be done quickly. I will give him some medicine at once, and meanwhile you must make some strong coffee."

"Coffee!" she exclaimed. "But we have none in the house. Will not tea do, if I make it very strong?"

"No, it will not. I must have coffee; and I must have it quickly."

"Then I suppose I must go and get some. But it is late. The shops will be shut. And I don't like leaving Mr. Graves."

"Can't you send the coachman?" I asked.

She shook her head impatiently. "No, that is no use. I must wait until Mr. Weiss comes."

"That won't do," I said, sharply. "He will slip through our fingers while you are waiting. You must go and get that coffee at once and bring it to me as soon as it is ready. And I want a tumbler and some water."

She brought me a water bottle and glass from the wash-stand and then with a groan of despair hurried from the room.

I lost no time in applying the remedies that I had at hand. Shaking out into the tumbler a few crystals of medicine, I filled it up with water and approached the patient. His stupor was profound. I shook him as roughly as was safe in his de-pressed condition, but that elicited no resistance or responsive movement. As it seemed very doubtful whether he was capable of swallowing, I dared not to take the risk of pouring the liquid into his mouth for fear of suffocating him. A stomach tube would have solved the difficulty, but I had none with me. I had, however, a mouth speculum which also acted as a gag, and having propped the patient's mouth open with this, I hastily slipped off one of the rubber tubes from my stethoscope and inserted a small funnel into one end of it. Then, introducing the other end of the tube into the gullet as far as its length would permit, I cautiously poured a small quantity of the medicine into the improvised funnel. To my great relief, a movement of the throat showed that the swallowing reflex still existed, and thus encouraged, I poured down the tube as much of the fluid as I thought it wise to administer at one time.

The dose of medicine that I had given was enough to neutralize any reasonable quantity of the poison that might yet remain in the stomach. I had next to deal with that portion of the drug which had already been absorbed and was exercising its poisonous effects. Taking my hypodermic case from my bag, I prepared in the syringe a full dose of atropine sulfate, which I injected forthwith into the unconscious man's arm. And that was all that I could do, so far as remedies were concerned, until the coffee arrived.

I cleaned and put away the syringe, washed the tube, and then returning to the bedside, endeavored to rouse the patient from his profound lethargy. But great care was necessary. A little carelessly rough handling, and that thready, flickering pulse might stop for ever. Yet it was almost certain that if he were not speedily aroused, his stupor would gradually deepen until it shaded off imperceptibly into death. I went to work very cautiously, moving his limbs about, flicking his face and chest with the corner of a wet towel, tickling the soles of his feet, and otherwise applying stimuli that were strong without being violent.

So occupied was I with my efforts to resuscitate my mysterious patient, that I did not notice the opening of the door. It was with something of a start that, happening to glance around, I perceived at the farther end of the room the shadowy figure of a man marked by two spots of light reflected from his spectacles. How long he had been watching me I cannot say, but when he saw that I had observed him, he came forward—though not very far—and I saw that he was Mr. Weiss.

"I am afraid," he said "that you do not find my friend so well tonight?"

"So well!" I exclaimed. "I don't find him well at all. I am exceedingly anxious about him."

"You don't . . . er . . . anticipate anything of a . . . er . . . anything serious, I hope?"

"There is no need to anticipate," said I. "It is already about as serious as it can be. I think he might die at any moment."

"You horrify me!" he gasped.

He was not exaggerating. In his agitation he stepped forward into the lighter part of the room, and I could see that his face was pale to ghastliness except for his nose and the adjacent red patches on his cheeks, which stood out in grotesquely hideous contrast. Presently, however, he recovered a little and said, "I really think—at least I hope—that you take an unnecessarily serious view of his condition. He has been like this before, you know."

I felt pretty certain that he had not, but there was no use in discussing the question. I therefore replied, as I continued my efforts to rouse the patient, "That may or may not be. But in any case there comes a last time, and it may have come now."

"I hope not," he said, "although I understand that these cases always end fatally sooner or later."

"What cases?" I asked.

"I was referring to sleeping sickness, but perhaps you have formed some other opinion as to the nature of this dreadful complaint."

I hesitated for a moment, and he continued, "As to your suggestion that his symptoms might be due to drugs, I think we may consider that false. He has been watched, practically without cessation since you came last, and I have myself turned out the room and examined the bed and have not found a trace of any drug. Have you gone into the question of sleeping sickness?"

I looked at the man narrowly before answering and distrusted him more than ever. But this was no time for reticence. My concern was with the patient and his present needs. After all, I was, as Thorndyke had said, a doctor, not a detective, and the circumstances called for straightforward speech and action on my part.

"I have considered that question," I said, "and have come to a perfectly definite conclusion. His symptoms are not those of sleeping sickness. They are in my opinion undoubtedly due to morphine poisoning."

"But, my dear sir," he exclaimed, "the thing is impossible! Haven't I just told you that he has been watched continuously?"

"I can only judge by the appearances that I find," I answered, and seeing that he was about to offer fresh objections, I continued, "Don't let us waste precious time in discussion, or Mr. Graves may he dead before we have reached a conclusion. If you will hurry them up about the coffee that I asked for some time ago, I will take the other necessary measures, and perhaps we may manage to pull him around."

The rather brutal decision of my manner evidently daunted him. It must have been plain to him that I was not prepared to accept any explanation of the unconscious man's condition other than that of morphine poisoning, whence the inference was pretty plain that the alternatives were recovery or an inquest. Replying stiffly that I "must do as I thought best," he hurried from the room, leaving me to continue my efforts without further interruption.

For some time these efforts seemed to make no impression. The man lay as still and impassive as a corpse excepting for the slow, shallow, and rather irregular breathing with its ominous accompanying rattle. But presently, by imperceptible degrees, signs of returning life began to make their appearance. A sharp slap on the cheek with the wet towel produced a sensible flicker of the eyelids; a similar slap on the chest was followed by a slight gasp. A pencil drawn over the sole of the foot occasioned a visible shrinking movement, and on looking once more at the eyes, I detected a slight change that told me that the atropine was beginning to take effect.

This was very encouraging, and so far, quite satisfactory, though it would have been premature to rejoice. I kept the patient carefully covered and maintained the process of gentle irritation, moving his limbs and shoulders, brushing his hair and generally bombarding his deadened senses with small but repeated stimuli. Under this treatment, the improvement continued so far that on my bawling a question into his ear, he actually opened his eyes for an instant, though in another moment, the lids had sunk back into their former position.

Soon after this Mr. Weiss reentered the room, followed by Mrs. Schallibaum, who carried a small tray, on which were a jug of coffee, a jug of milk, a cup and saucer and a sugar bowl.

"How do you find him now?" Mr. Weiss asked anxiously.

"I am glad to say that there is a distinct improvement," I replied. "But we must persevere. He is by no means out of the wood yet."

I examined the coffee, which looked black and strong and had a very reassuring smell, and pouring out half a cupful, approached the bed.

"Now, Mr. Graves," I shouted, "we want you to drink some of this."

The flaccid eyelids lifted for an instant, but there was no other response. I gently opened the unresisting mouth and ladled in a couple of spoonfuls of coffee, which were immediately swallowed; whereupon I repeated the process and continued at short intervals until the cup was empty. The effect of the new remedy soon became apparent. He began to mumble and mutter obscurely in response to the questions that I bellowed at him, and once or twice he opened his eyes and looked dreamily into my face. Then I sat him up and made him drink some coffee from the cup, and all the time kept up a running fire of questions, which made up in volume of sound for what they lacked of relevancy.

Of these proceedings Mr. Weiss and his housekeeper were highly interested spectators, and the former, contrary to his usual practice, came quite close up to the bed to get a better view.

"It is really a most remarkable thing," he said, "but it almost looks as if you were right, after all. He is certainly much better. But tell me, would this treatment produce a similar improvement if the symptoms were due to disease?"

"No," I answered, "it certainly would not."

"Then that seems to settle it. But it is a most mysterious affair. Can you suggest any way in which he can have concealed a store of the drug?"

I stood up and looked him straight in the face. It was the first chance I had had of inspecting him by any but the feeblest light, and I looked at him very attentively. Now it is a curious fact that there sometimes occurs a considerable interval between the reception of a visual impression and its complete transfer to the consciousness. A thing may be seen, as it were, unconsciously, and the impression apparently consigned to instant oblivion; and yet the picture may be subsequently revived by memory with such completeness that its details can be studied as though the object were still actually visible.

Something of this kind must have happened to me now. Preoccupied as I was by the condition of the patient, the professional habit of rapid and close observation caused me to direct a searching glance at the man before me. It was only a brief glance for Mr. Weiss, perhaps embarrassed by my keen regard of him, almost immediately withdrew into the shadow. My attention seemed principally to be occupied by the odd contrast between the pallor of his face and the redness of his nose and by the peculiar stiff, bristly character of his eyebrows. But there was another fact, and a very curious one, that was observed by me subconsciously and instantly forgotten, to be revived later when I reflected on the events of the night. It was this.

As Mr. Weiss stood, with his head slightly turned, I was able to look through one glass of his spectacles at the wall beyond. On the wall was a framed print; and the edge of the frame, seen through the eyeglass, appeared quite unaltered and free from distortion, magnification, or reduction. It was like seeing through plain window glass, and yet the reflections of the candle flame in the spectacles showed the flame upside down, proving conclusively that the glasses were concave on one surface at least. The strange phenomenon was visible only for a moment or two, and as it passed out of my sight it passed also out of my mind.

"No," I said, replying to the last question, "I can think of no way in which he could have effectually hidden a store of morphine. Judging by the symptoms, he has taken a large dose, and if he has been in the habit of consuming large quantities, his stock would be pretty bulky. I can offer no suggestion whatever."

"I suppose you consider him quite out of danger now?"

"Oh, not at all. I think we can pull him around if we persevere, but he must not be allowed to sink back into a state of coma. We must keep him on the move until the effects of the drug have really passed off. If you will put him into his dressing gown, we will walk him up and down the room for a while."

"But is that safe?" Mr. Weiss asked anxiously.

"Quite safe," I answered. "I will watch his pulse carefully. The danger is in the certainty of a relapse if he is not kept moving."

With obvious unwillingness and disapproval, Mr. Weiss produced a dressing gown and together we invested the patient in it. Then we dragged him, very limp but not entirely unre-sisting, out of bed and stood him on his feet. He opened his eyes and blinked owlishly first at one and then at the other of us, and mumbled a few unintelligible words of protest, regardless of which, we thrust his feet into slippers and endeavored to make him walk. At first he seemed unable to stand, and we had to support him by his arms as we urged him forward. But presently his trailing legs began to make definite walking movements, and after one or two turns up and down the room, he was not only able partly to support his weight, but showed evidence of reviving consciousness in more energetic protests.

At this point Mr. Weiss astonished me by transferring the arm that he held to the housekeeper.

"If you will excuse me, Doctor," said he, "I will go now and attend to some rather important business that I have had to leave unfinished. Mrs. Schallibaum will be able to give you all the assistance that you require and will order the carriage when you think it safe to leave the patient. In case I should not see you again, I will say good night. I hope you won't think me ungrateful."

He shook hands with me and went out of the room, leaving me, as I have said, profoundly astonished that he should consider any business of more importance than the condition of his friend, whose life, even now, was but hanging by a thread. However, it was really no concern of mine. I could do without him, and the resuscitation of this unfortunate man gave me occupation enough to engross my whole attention.

The slow progress up and down the room recommenced, and with it the mumbled protests from the patient. As we walked, and especially as we turned, I caught frequent glimpses of the housekeeper's face, but it was nearly always in profile. She appeared to avoid looking me in the face, though she did so once or twice, and on each of these occasions her eyes were directed at me in a normal manner without any sign of a squint. Nevertheless, I had the impression that when her face was turned away from me she squinted. The "swivel eye"—the left—was towards me as she held the patient's right arm, and it was almost continuously turned in my direction, whereas I felt convinced that she was really looking straight before her, though, of course, her right eye was invisible to me. It struck me even at the time as an odd affair, but I was too much concerned about my charge to give it much consideration.

Meanwhile the patient continued to revive apace. And the more he revived, the more energetically did he protest against this wearisome perambulation. But he was evidently a polite gentleman for, muddled as his faculties were, he managed to clothe his objections in courteous and even gracious forms of speech singularly out of agreement with the character that Mr. Weiss had given him.

"I thangyou," he mumbled thickly. "Ver' good take s'much trouble. Think I will lie down now." He looked wistfully at the bed, but I wheeled him about and marched him once more down the room. He submitted unresistingly, but as we again approached the bed he reopened the matter.

"S'quite s'fficient, thang you. Gebback to bed now. Much 'bliged frall your kindness"—here I turned him around—"no, really. M'feeling rather tired. Sh'like to lie down now, f'you'd be s'good."

"You must walk about a little longer, Mr. Graves," I said. "It would be very bad for you to go to sleep again."

He looked at me with a curious, dull surprise, and reflected awhile as if in some perplexity. Then he looked at me again and said, "Thing, sir, you are mistake—mistaken me—mist—"

Here Mrs. Schallibaum interrupted sharply, "The doctor thinks it's good for you to walk about. You've been sleeping too much. He doesn't want you to sleep any more just now."

"Don't wanter sleep; wanter lie down," said the patient.

"But you mustn't lie down for a little while. You must walk about for a few minutes more. And you'd better not talk. Just walk up and down."

"There's no harm in his talking," said I, "in fact it's good for him. It will help to keep him awake."

"I should think it would tire him," said Mrs. Schallibaum, "and it worries me to hear him asking to lie down when we can't let him."

She spoke sharply and in an unnecessarily high tone so that the patient could not fail to hear. Apparently he took in the very broad hint contained in the concluding sentence, for he trudged wearily and unsteadily up and down the room for some time without speaking, though he continued to look at me from time to time as if something in my appearance puzzled him exceedingly. At length his intolerable longing for repose overcame his politeness, and he returned to the attack.

"Surely v' walked enough now. Feeling very tired. Am really. Would you be s'kind 's t'let me lie down few minutes?"

"Don't you think he might lie down for a little while?" Mrs. Schallibaum asked.

I felt his pulse and decided that he was really becoming fatigued and that it would be wiser not to overdo the exercise while he was so weak.

Accordingly, I consented to his returning to bed and turned him around in that direction, whereupon he tottered gleefully towards his resting place like a tired horse heading for its stable.

As soon as he was tucked in, I gave him a full cup of coffee, which he drank with some avidity as if thirsty. Then I sat down by the bedside, and with a view to keeping him awake, began once more to ply him with questions.

"Does your head ache, Mr. Graves?" I asked.

"The doctor says 'does your head ache?'" Mrs. Schallibaum squalled, so loudly that the patient started perceptibly.

"I heard him, m'dear girl," he answered with a faint smile. "Not deaf, you know. Yes. Head aches a good deal. But I thing this gennleman mistakes—"

"He says you are to keep awake. You mustn't go to sleep again, and you are not to close your eyes."

"All ri' Pol'n. Keep'm open," and he proceeded forthwith to shut them with an air of infinite peacefulness. I grasped his hand and shook it gently, on which he opened his eyes and looked at me sleepily. The housekeeper stroked his head, keeping her face half-turned from me as she had done almost constantly, to conceal the squinting eye I assumed, and said, "Need we keep you any longer, Doctor? It is getting very late and you have a long way to go."

I looked doubtfully at the patient. I was loath to leave him, distrusting these people as I did. But I had my work to do on the morrow with perhaps a night call or two in the interval, and the endurance even of a general practitioner has its limits.

"I think I heard the carriage some time ago," Mrs. Schallibaum added.

I rose hesitatingly and looked at my watch. It had turned half-past eleven.

"You understand," I said in a low voice, "that the danger is not over? If he is left now, he will fall asleep, and in all human probability will never wake. You clearly understand that?"

"Yes, quite clearly. I promise you he shall not be allowed to fall asleep again."

As she spoke, she looked me full in the face for a few moments, and I noted that her eyes had a perfectly normal appearance, without any trace whatever of a squint.

"Very well," I said. "On that understanding I will go now, and I shall hope to find our friend quite recovered at my next visit."

I turned to the patient, who was already dozing, and shook his hand heartily.

"Goodbye, Mr. Graves!" I said. "I am sorry to have had to disturb your repose so much, but you must keep awake, you know. Won't do to go to sleep."

"Ver' well," he replied drowsily. "Sorry t' give you all this trouble. L' keep awake. But I think you're mistak'n—"

"He says it's very important that you shouldn't go to sleep, and that I am to see that you don't. Do you understand?"

"Yes, I un'stan'. But why does this gennlem'n—"

"Now it's of no use for you to ask a lot of questions," Mrs. Schallibaum said playfully; "we'll talk to you tomorrow. Good night, Doctor. I'll light you down the stairs, but I won't come down with you, or the patient will be falling asleep again."

Taking this definite dismissal, I retired, followed by a dreamily surprised glance from the sick man. The housekeeper held the candle over the balusters until I reached the bottom of the stairs, when I perceived through the open door along the passage a glimmer of light from the carriage lamps. The coachman was standing just outside, faintly illuminated by the very dim lamplight, and as I stepped into the carriage he remarked in his Scotch dialect that I "seemed to have been makin' a night of it." He did not wait for any reply—none being in fact needed—but shut the door and locked it.

I lit my little pocket lamp and hung it on the back cushion. I even drew the board and notebook from my pocket. But it seemed rather unnecessary to take a fresh set of notes, and to tell the truth, I rather shirked the labor, tired as I was after my late exertions. Besides, I wanted to think over the events of the evening while they were fresh in my memory. Accordingly I put away the notebook and settled myself to review the incidents attending my second visit to this rather uncanny house.

Considered in leisurely retrospect, that visit offered quite a number of problems that called for explanation. There was the patient's condition, for instance. Any doubt as to the cause of his symptoms was set at rest by the effect of the antidotes. Mr. Graves was certainly under the influence of morphine, and the only doubtful question was how he had become so. That he had taken the poison himself was incredible. It was practically certain that the poison had been administered by someone else, and on Mr. Weiss's own word, there was no one but himself and the housekeeper who could have administered it. And to this conclusion all the other very queer circumstances pointed.

They were, as I have said, numerous, though many of them seemed trivial. To begin with, Mr. Weiss's habit of appearing sometime after my arrival and disappearing sometime before my departure was decidedly odd. But still odder was his sudden departure this evening on what looked like a mere pretext. That departure coincided in time with the sick man's recovery of the power of speech. Could it be that Mr. Weiss was afraid that the half-conscious man might say something compromising to him in my presence? It looked rather like it. And yet he had gone away and left me with the patient and the housekeeper.

But when I came to think about it, I remembered that Mrs. Schallibaum had shown some anxiety to prevent the patient from talking. She had interrupted him more than once and had on two occasions broken in when he seemed to be about to ask me some question. I was "mistaken" about something. What was that something that he wanted to tell me?

It had struck me as singular that there should be no coffee in the house, but a sufficiency of tea. Germans are not usually tea drinkers, and they do take coffee. But perhaps there was nothing in this. Rather more remarkable was the invisibility of the coachman. Why could he not be sent to fetch the coffee, and why did not he, rather than the housekeeper, come to take the place of Mr. Weiss when the latter had to go away?

There were other points too. I recalled the word that sounded like "Pol'n," which Mr. Graves had used in speaking to the housekeeper. Apparently it was a Christian name of some kind, but why did Mr. Graves call the woman by her Christian name when Mr. Weiss addressed her formally as Mrs. Schallibaum? And as to the woman herself, what was the meaning of that curious disappearing squint? Physically it presented no mystery. The woman had an ordinary divergent squint, and like many people who suffer from this displacement, she could, by a strong muscular effort, bring the eyes temporarily into their normal parallel position. But why had she done so? Was it only feminine vanity—mere sensitiveness respecting a slight personal disfigurement? It might be so, or there might be some further motive. It was impossible to say.

Turning this question over, I suddenly remembered the peculiarity of Mr. Weiss's spectacles. And here I met with a real puzzle. I had certainly seen through those spectacles as clearly as if they had been plain window glass. And they had certainly given an inverted reflection of the candle flame like that thrown from the surface of a concave lens. They obviously could not be both flat and concave, yet they had the properties peculiar to both flatness and concavity. And there was a further difficulty. If I could see objects unaltered through them, so could Mr. Weiss. But the function of spectacles is to alter the appearances of objects, by magnification, reduction, or compensating distortion. If they leave the appearances unchanged, they are useless. I could make nothing of it. After puzzling over it for quite a long time, I had to give it up, inasmuch as the construction of Mr. Weiss's spectacles had no apparent bearing on the case.

On arriving home, I looked anxiously at the message book and was relieved to find that there were no further visits to be made. Having made up a mixture for Mr. Graves and handed it to the coachman, I raked the ashes of the surgery fire together and sat down to reflect once more on this suspicious case in which I had become involved. Fatigue soon put an end to my meditations, and having come to the conclusion that the circumstances demanded a further consultation with Thorndyke, I turned down the gas and took myself to bed.

CHAPTER 4
THE OFFICIAL VIEW

I rose on the following morning still determined to find an opportunity during the day to call on Thorndyke and get his advice on the now urgent question as to what I was to do. I use the word "urgent" advisedly, for the incidents of the preceding evening had left me with the firm conviction that poison was being administered for some purpose to my mysterious patient, and that no time must be lost if his life was to be saved. Last night he had escaped only by the narrowest margin—assuming him to be still alive—and it was only my firm attitude that had compelled Mr. Weiss to agree to restorative measures.

That I should be sent for again I had not the slightest expectation. If what I so strongly suspected was true, Weiss would call in some other doctor, and it was imperative that he should be stopped before it was too late. This was my view, but I meant to have Thorndyke's opinion and act under his direction.

When I came downstairs and took a preliminary glance at the message book kept by the apothecary's assistant, I stood aghast. The morning's entries looked already like a sample page of the post office directory. The new calls alone were more than equal to an ordinary day's work, and the routine visits remained to be added. Gloomily wondering whether the Black Death had made a sudden reappearance in England, I hurried to the dining room and made a hasty breakfast, interrupted at intervals by the appearance of said assistant to announce new messages.

The first two or three visits solved the mystery. An epidemic of influenza had descended on the neighborhood, and I was getting not only our own normal work but a certain amount of overflow from other practices.

Of course my visit to Thorndyke was now out of the question. I would have to act on my own instincts. But in the hurry and rush and anxiety of the work—for some of the cases were severe—I had no opportunity to consider any course of action, nor time to figure it out. Even with the aid of a cab which I chartered, as Stillbury kept no carriage, I had not finished my last visit until near to midnight and was then so fatigued that I fell asleep over my postponed supper.

As the next day opened with a further increase of work, I sent a telegram to Dr. Stillbury at Hastings, where he had gone to recuperate after a slight illness. I asked for authority to engage an assistant, but the reply informed me that Stillbury himself was on his way to town. To my relief, when I dropped in at the surgery for a cup of tea, I found him rubbing his hands over the open day book.

"It's an ill wind that blows nobody good," he remarked cheerfully as we shook hands. "This will pay the expenses of my holiday, including your salary. By the way, you are not anxious to be off, I suppose?"

As a matter of fact, I was, for I had decided to accept Thorndyke's offer and was now eager to take up my duties with him. But it would have been shabby to leave Stillbury to battle alone with this rush of work or to seek the services of a strange assistant.

"I should like to get off as soon as you can spare me," I replied, "but I'm not going to leave you in the lurch."

"That's a good fellow," said Stillbury. "I knew you wouldn't. Let us have some tea and divide up the work. Anything of interest going?"

There were one or two unusual cases on the list, and as we marked off our respective patients, I gave him the histories in brief synopsis. And then I opened the subject of my mysterious experiences at the house of Mr. Weiss.

"There's another affair that I want to tell you about; rather an unpleasant business."

"Oh, dear!" exclaimed Stillbury. He put down his cup and regarded me with quite painful anxiety.

"It looks to me undoubtedly like a case of criminal poisoning," I continued.

Stillbury's face cleared instantly. "Oh, I'm glad it's nothing more than that," he said with an air of relief. "There's always the danger of romance, you know, when the doctor is young and happens—if I may say so, Jervis—to be a good-looking fellow. Then let us hear about this case."

I gave him a condensed narrative of my connection with the mysterious patient, omitting any reference to Thorndyke and passing lightly over my efforts to fix the position of the house, and wound up with the remark that the facts ought certainly to be communicated to the police.

"Yes," he admitted reluctantly, "I suppose you're right. Surely unpleasant though. Police cases don't do a practice any good. They waste a lot of time too; keep you hanging about to give evidence. Still, you are quite right. We can't stand by and see the poor devil poisoned without making some effort. But I don't believe the police will do anything in the matter."

"Don't you really?"

"No, I don't. They like to have things pretty well cut-and-dried before they act. A prosecution is an expensive affair, so they don't care to prosecute unless they are fairly sure of a conviction."

"But don't you think they would get a conviction in this case?"

"Not on your evidence, Jervis. You haven't got enough hard-baked facts to upset a capable defense. Still, that isn't our affair. You want to put the responsibility on the police, and I entirely agree with you."

"There ought not to be any delay," said I.

"There needn't be. I shall look in on Mrs. Wackford, and you have to see the Rummel children. We shall pass the station on our way. Why don't we just drop in and see the inspector?"

The suggestion met my views exactly. As soon as we had finished tea, we set forth, and in about ten minutes found ourselves in the bare and forbidding office attached to the station.

The presiding officer descended from a high stool and, carefully laying down his pen, shook hands cordially.

"And what can I do for you gentlemen?" he asked with an affable smile.

Stillbury proceeded to open our business.

"My friend here, Dr. Jervis, who has very kindly been looking after my practice for a week or two, has had a most remarkable experience, and he wants to tell you about it."

"Something in my line of business?" the officer inquired.

"That," said I, "is for you to judge. I think it is, but you may think otherwise," and hereupon, without further preamble, I plunged into the history of the case, giving him a condensed statement similar to that which I had already made to Stillbury.

He listened with close attention, jotting down from time to time a brief note on a sheet of paper; and when I had finished, he wrote out in a black-covered notebook a short summary of my statement.

"I have written down here," he said, "the substance of what you have told me. I will read the deposition back to you, and if it is correct, I will ask you to sign it."

He did so, and when I had signed the document, I asked him what was likely to be done in the matter.

"I am afraid," he replied, "that we can't take any active measures. You have put us on our guard, and we shall keep our eyes open. But I think that is all we can do unless we hear something further."

"But," I exclaimed, "don't you think that it is a very suspicious affair?"

"I do," he replied. "A very fishy business indeed, and you were quite right to come and tell us about it."

"It seems a pity not to take some measures," I said. "While you are waiting to hear something further, they may give the poor wretch a fresh dose and kill him."

"In which case we should hear something further, unless some fool of a doctor were to give a death certificate."

"But that is very unsatisfactory. The man ought not to be allowed to die."

"I quite agree with you, sir. But we've no evidence that he is going to die. His friends sent for you, and you treated him skillfully and left him on the way to recovery. That's all that we really know about it. Yes, I know," the officer continued as I made signs of disagreement, "you think that a crime is possibly going to be committed and that we ought to prevent it. You overrate our powers. We can only act on evidence that a crime has actually been committed or is actually being attempted. We have no such evidence. Look at your statement, and tell me what you can swear to."

"I think I could swear that Mr. Graves had taken a poisonous dose of morphine."

"And who gave him that poisonous dose?"

"I very strongly suspect—"

"That's no good, sir," interrupted the officer. "Suspicion isn't evidence. We would want you to give us enough facts to make out a bona fide case against some definite person. And you can't do it. Your information amounts to this: that a certain person has taken a poisonous dose of morphine and apparently recovered. That's all. You can't swear that the names given to you are real names, and you can't give us any address or even any locality."

"I took some compass bearings in the carriage," I said. "You could locate the house, I think, without much difficulty."

The officer smiled faintly and fixed an abstracted gaze on the clock.

"You could, sir," he replied. "I have no doubt whatever that *you* could. I couldn't. We simply haven't enough to go upon. If you learn anything new, I hope you will let me know, and I am very much obliged to you for taking so much trouble in the matter. Good evening, sir. Good evening, Dr. Stillbury."

He shook hands with us both genially, and accepting this very polite but unmistakable dismissal, we took our departure.

Outside the station, Stillbury heaved a comfortable sigh. He was evidently relieved to find that no upheavals were to take place in his domain.

"I thought that would be their attitude," he said, "and they are quite right, you know. The function of law is to prevent crime, it is true, but prevention in the sense in which we understand it is not possible in legal practice."

I agreed without enthusiasm. It was disappointing to find that no precautionary measures were to be taken. However, I had done all that I could in the matter. No further responsibility lay upon me, and as it was practically certain that I had seen and heard the last of Mr. Graves and his mysterious household, I dismissed the case from my mind. At the next corner Stillbury and I parted to go our respective ways, and my attention was soon transferred from the romance of crime to the realities of epidemic influenza.

The volume of work in Dr. Stillbury's practice continued longer than I had bargained for. Day after day went by and still found me tramping the dingy streets of Kennington or scrambling up and down narrow stairways.

It was very provoking. For months I had resisted Thorndyke's persuasion to give up general practice and join him. Not from lack of inclination, but from a deep suspicion that he was thinking of my wants, rather than his own; that his was a charitable rather than a business proposal. Now that I knew this not to be the case, I was impatient to join him. As I trudged through this outdated suburb, with its once rustic villas and its faded gardens, my thoughts would turn enviously to the quiet dignity of the Temple and my friend's chambers in King's Bench Walk.

The closed carriage appeared no more; nor did any whisper either of good or evil reach me in connection with the mysterious house from which it had come. Mr. Graves had apparently gone out of my life forever.

But if he had gone out of my life, he had not gone out of my memory. Often as I walked my rounds would the picture of that dimly lit room rise unbidden. Often would I find myself looking once more into that ghastly face, so worn, wasted, and haggard, and yet so far from repellent. All the incidents of that last night would reconstitute themselves with a vividness that showed the intensity of the impression that they had made at the time. I would have gladly forgotten the whole affair, for every incident of it was fraught with discomfort. But it clung to my memory; it haunted me; and ever as it returned, it bore with it the disquieting questions: was Mr. Graves still alive? And if he was not, was there really nothing that could have been done to save him?

Nearly a month passed before the practice began to show signs of returning to its normal condition. Then the daily lists became more and more contracted, and the day's work proportionately shorter. And thus the term of my servitude came to an end.

One evening as we were writing up the daybook, Stillbury remarked, "I almost think, Jervis, I could manage by myself now. I know you are only staying on for my sake."

"I am staying on to finish my engagement, but I shan't be sorry to clear out if you can do without me."

"I think I can. When would you like to be off?"

"As soon as possible. Say tomorrow morning after I have made a few visits and transferred the patients to you."

"Very well," said Stillbury. "Then I will give you your check and settle up everything tonight, so that you shall be free to go off when you like tomorrow morning."

Thus ended my connection with Kennington Lane. On the following day at about noon, I found myself strolling across Waterloo Bridge with the sensations of a newly liberated convict and a check for my services in my pocket.

My luggage was to follow when I sent for it. Now unhampered even by a handbag, I joyfully descended the steps at the north end of the bridge and headed for King's Bench Walk by way of the Embankment and Middle Temple Lane.

CHAPTER 5
JEFFREY BLACKMORE'S WILL

My arrival at Thorndyke's chambers was not unexpected. The door was open and an application of the little brass knocker to the inner door immediately produced my colleague himself and a very hearty welcome.

"At last," said Thorndyke, "you have come forth from the house of bondage. I began to think that you had taken up your abode in Kennington for good."

"I was beginning to wonder myself when I should escape. But here I am, and I may say at once that I am ready to shake the dust of general practice off my feet forever—that is, if you are still willing to have me as your assistant."

"Willing!" exclaimed Thorndyke, "You will be invaluable to me. Let us settle the terms of our partnership, and tomorrow we will begin. Shall we have our talk in the open air and the spring sunshine?"

I agreed readily to this proposal, for it was a bright, sunny day and warm for the beginning of April. We descended to the Walk and then slowly made our way to the quiet court behind the church. I need not record the matter of our conversation. To Thorndyke's proposals I had no objections to offer but my own unworthiness and his excessive liberality. A few minutes saw our covenants fully agreed upon, and when Thorndyke had noted the points on a slip of paper, signed and dated it and handed it to me, the business was at an end.

"There," my colleague said with a smile as he put away his pocketbook, "if people would only settle their affairs in that way, a good part of the occupation of lawyers would be gone."

"And now," I said, "I propose that we go and feed. I will invite you to lunch to celebrate our contract."

"My learned junior is premature," he replied, "I have already arranged a little festivity—or rather have modified one that was already arranged. You remember Mr. Marchmont, the solicitor?"

"Yes."

"He called this morning to ask me to lunch with him and a new client at the Cheshire Cheese. I accepted and notified him that I should bring you."

"Why the Cheshire Cheese?" I asked.

"Why not? Marchmont's reasons for the selection were, first, that his client has never seen an old-fashioned London tavern, and second, that this is Wednesday and he, Marchmont, has a gluttonous affection for a really fine beef steak pudding. You don't object, I hope."

"Oh, not at all. In fact, now that you mention it, my own sensations incline me to sympathize with Marchmont. I breakfasted rather early."

"Then come," said Thorndyke. "The reservation is for one o'clock, and if we walk slowly, we shall just arrive in time."

We sauntered up Inner Temple Lane and, crossing Fleet Street, headed sedately for the tavern. As we entered the quaint, old-world dining room, Thorndyke looked around and a gentleman who was seated with a companion at a table in one of the little compartments rose and saluted us.

"Let me introduce you to my friend, Mr. Stephen Blackmore," he said as we approached. Then turning to his companion, he introduced us by our respective names.

"I engaged this table," he continued, "so that we might be private if we wished to have a little preliminary chat, not that beef steak pudding is a great help to conversation. But when people have a certain business in view, their talk is sure to drift towards it, sooner or later."

Thorndyke and I sat down opposite the lawyer and his client, and we mutually inspected one another. I knew Marchmont already. He was an elderly, professional-looking man, a typical solicitor of the old school, fresh faced, precise, rather irascible, and conveying a not unpleasant impression of taking a reasonable interest in his diet. The other man was quite young, not more than twenty-five, and was a fine athletic-looking fellow with a healthy, out-of-door complexion and an intelligent and handsome face. I took a liking to him at the first glance, and so, I saw, did Thorndyke.

"You two gentlemen," said Blackmore, addressing us, "seem to be quite old acquaintances. I have heard so much about you from my friend, Reuben Hornby."

"Ah, yes!" exclaimed Marchmont, "Your work is an eye opener to old-fashioned lawyers like myself. The scientific lawyer is something new. Your appearance in court has made us all sit up, I can assure you."

"I hope we shall make you sit up again," said Thorndyke.

"You won't this time," said Marchmont. "The issues in this case of Blackmore's are purely legal; or rather, there are no issues at all. There is nothing in dispute. I tried to prevent Blackmore from consulting you, but he wouldn't listen to reason. Here! Waiter! How much longer are *we* to be waiters? We shall die of old age before we get our victuals!"

The waiter smiled apologetically. "Yes, sir," said he. "Coming now, sir."

And at this very moment there was borne into the room a gargantuan platter, which being placed on a three-legged stool was forthwith attacked ferociously by the white clothed, white capped carver. We watched the process—as did everyone present—with an interest not entirely gluttonous, for it added a pleasant touch to the picturesque old room with its sanded floor, its homely, pew-like boxes, its high backed settles, and the friendly portrait that beamed down on us from the wall.

"This is a very different affair from your great, glittering modern restaurants," Mr. Marchmont remarked.

"It is indeed," said Blackmore, "and if this is the way in which our ancestors lived, it would seem that they had a better idea of comfort than we have."

There was a short pause, during which Mr. Marchmont glared hungrily at the platter, then Thorndyke said, "So you refused to listen to reason, Mr. Blackmore?"

"Yes. You see, Mr. Marchmont and his partner had gone into the matter and decided that there was nothing to be done. Then I happened to mention the affair to Reuben Hornby, and he urged me to take your advice on the case."

"Just like him," growled Marchmont, "to meddle with my client."

"I spoke to Mr. Marchmont," continued Blackmore, "and he agreed that it was worth while to take your opinion on the case though he warned me to cherish no hopes, as the affair was not really within your specialty."

"So you understand," said Marchmont, "that we expect nothing. We are taking your opinion as a mere formality to be able to say that we have left nothing untried."

"That is an encouraging start," Thorndyke remarked. "It leaves me unembarrassed by the possibility of failure. But meanwhile you are arousing in me some curiosity as to the nature of the case. Is it highly confidential? Because if not, I would mention that Jervis has now joined me as my permanent colleague."

"It isn't confidential at all," said Marchmont. "The public are in full possession of the fact, and we should be only too happy to put them in still fuller possession through the medium of the probate court, if we could find a reasonable pretext. But we can't."

Here the waiter charged our table with the fussy rapidity of the overdue.

"Sorry to keep you waiting, sir. Wouldn't like it underdone, sir."

Marchmont inspected his plate critically and remarked, "I sometimes suspect these oysters of being mussels, and I'll swear the larks are sparrows."

"Let us hope so," said Thorndyke. "The lark is better employed at Heaven's gate singing than garnishing a beef steak pudding. But you were telling us about your case."

"So I was. Well it's just a matter of a perverse testator and an ill-drawn will. A peculiarly irritating case too, because the defective will replaces a perfectly sound one," said the unabashed solicitor. "But business is business, and eating is eating; let us eat now and talk over our case in my office or your chambers after lunch."

"Yes," said Thorndyke, "come over to the Temple with me, and I will give you a cup of coffee to clear your brain. Are there any documents?"

"I have all the papers here in my bag," replied Marchmont, and the conversation drifted into other channels.

As soon as the meal was finished and the reckoning paid, we trooped out and pushed ourselves through the line of empty cabs that crawled in a continuous procession on either side of Fleet Street. We took ourselves by way of Mitre Court to King's Bench Walk. There, when the coffee had been requested and our chairs drawn up around the fire, Mr. Marchmont unloaded from his bag a bundle of papers, and we addressed ourselves to the business at hand.

"Now," said Marchmont, "let me repeat what I said before. Legally speaking, we have no case—not the ghost of one. But my client wished to take your opinion, and I agreed on the bare chance that you might detect some point that we had overlooked. I don't think you will, for we have gone into the case very thoroughly, but still there is the infinitesimal chance, and we may as well take it. Would you like to read the two wills, or shall I first explain the circumstances?"

"I think," replied Thorndyke, "a narrative of the events in the order of their occurrence would be most helpful. I should like to know as much as possible about the testator before I examine the documents."

"Very well," said Marchmont. "Then I will begin with a recital of the circumstances, which briefly stated are these: My client, Stephen Blackmore, is the son of Mr. Edward Blackmore, deceased; Edward Blackmore had two brothers who survived him, John, the elder, and Jeffrey, the younger; Jeffrey is the testator in this case.

"Some two years ago, Jeffrey Blackmore executed a will by which he made his nephew Stephen his executor and sole beneficiary, and a few months later he added a codicil giving two hundred and fifty pounds to his brother John."

"What was the value of the estate?" Thorndyke asked.

"About three thousand five hundred pounds, all invested. The testator had a pension from the Foreign Office on which he lived, leaving his capital untouched. Soon after having made his will, he left the rooms in Jermyn Street where he had lived for some years, stored his furniture, and went to Florence. From thence he moved on to Rome and then to Venice and other places in Italy, and so continued to travel about until the end of last September, when it appears that he returned to England. At the beginning of October he took a set of rooms in New Inn, which he furnished with some of the things from his old rooms. As far as we can make out, he never communicated with any of his friends, except for his brother. The fact of his being in residence at Number 31, New Inn, or of his being in England at all, became known to them only when he died."

"Was this quite in accordance with his ordinary habits?" Thorndyke asked.

"I should say not," Blackmore answered.

"My uncle was a studious, solitary man, but he was not formerly a recluse. He was not much of a correspondent, but he kept up some sort of communication with his friends. For instance, he used to write to me on occasion, and when I came down from Cambridge for vacations, he had me to stay with him at his rooms."

"Is there anything known that accounts for the change in his habits?"

"Yes, there is," replied Marchmont. "We shall come to that presently. To proceed with the narrative. On the fifteenth of last March he was found dead in his chambers, and a more recent will was then discovered, dated the twelfth of November of last year. Now, no change had taken place in the circumstances of the testator to account for the new will, nor was there any appreciable alteration in the disposition of the property. As far as we can make out, the new will was drawn with the idea of stating the intentions of the testator with greater exactness and for the sake of doing away with the codicil. The entire property, with the exception of two hundred and fifty pounds was, as before, bequeathed to Stephen, but the separate items were specified, and the testator's brother, John Blackmore, was named as the executor and sole beneficiary."

"I see," said Thorndyke. "So that your client's interest in the will would appear to be practically unaffected by the change."

"Yes. There it is," exclaimed the lawyer, slapping the table to add emphasis to his words. "That is the pity of it! If people who have no knowledge of law would only refrain from tinkering at their wills, what a world of trouble would be saved!"

"Oh, come," said Thorndyke. "It is not for a lawyer to say that."

"No, I suppose not," Marchmont agreed. "Only, you see, we like the muddle to be made by the other side. But in this case, the muddle is on our side. The change, as you say, seems to leave our friend Stephen's interests unaffected. That is, of course, what poor Jeffrey Blackmore thought. But he was mistaken. The effect of the change is absolutely disastrous."

"Indeed?"

"Yes. As I have said, no alteration in the testator's circumstances had taken place at the time the new will was executed. But only two days before his death, his sister, Mrs. Edmund Wilson, died. On her will being proved, it appeared that she had bequeathed to him her entire worth."

"Heigh-o!" exclaimed Thorndyke. "What an unfortunate affair!"

"You are right," said Mr. Marchmont. "By the original will, this great sum would have accrued to our friend Mr. Stephen, whereas now, of course, it goes to the beneficiary, Mr. John Blackmore. And what makes it even more exasperating is the fact that this is obviously not in accordance with the wishes and intentions of Mr. Jeffrey, who clearly desired his nephew to inherit his property."

"Yes. I think you are justified in assuming that. Do you know whether Mr. Jeffrey was aware of his sister's intention?"

"We think not. Her will was executed as recently as the third of September last, and it seems that there had been no communication between her and Mr. Jeffrey since that date. Besides, if you consider Mr. Jeffrey's actions, you will see that they suggest no knowledge or expectation of this very important bequest. A man does not make elaborate dispositions in regard to three thousand pounds and then leave a sum of thirty thousand to be disposed of casually as the residue of the estate."

"No," Thorndyke agreed. "And, as you have said, the manifest intention of the testator was to leave the bulk of his property to Mr. Stephen. So we may take it as virtually certain that Mr. Jeffrey had no knowledge of the fact that he was a beneficiary under his sister's will."

"Yes," said Mr. Marchmont, "I think we may take that as nearly certain."

"With reference to the second will," said Thorndyke, "I suppose there is no need to ask whether the document itself has been examined; I mean as to its being a genuine document and perfectly regular?"

Mr. Marchmont shook his head sadly.

"No," he said, "I am sorry to say that there can be no possible doubt as to the authenticity and regularity of the document. The circumstances under which it was executed establish its genuineness beyond any question."

"What were those circumstances?" Thorndyke asked.

"They were these: On the morning of the twelfth of November last, Mr. Jeffrey came to the porter's lodge with a document in his hand. 'This,' he said 'is my will. I want you to witness my signature. Would you mind doing so? Can you find another respectable person to act as the second witness?' Now it happened that a nephew of the porter's, a painter by trade, was at work in the inn. The porter went out and fetched him into the lodge, and the two men agreed to witness the signature. 'You better read the will,' said Mr. Jeffrey. 'It is not actually necessary, but it is an additional safeguard, and there is nothing of a private nature in the document.' The two men accordingly read the document, and when Mr. Jeffrey had signed it in their presence, they affixed their signatures. And I may add that the painter left the recognizable impressions of three greasy fingers."

"And these witnesses have been examined?"

"Yes. They have both sworn to the document and to their own signatures, and the painter recognized his finger marks."

"That," said Thorndyke, "seems to dispose pretty effectually of any question as to the genuineness of the will; and if, as I gather, Mr. Jeffrey came to the lodge alone, the question of undue influence is disposed of too."

"Yes," said Mr. Marchmont. "I think we must pass the will as absolutely flawless."

"It strikes me as rather odd," said Thorndyke, "that Jeffrey should have known so little about his sister's intentions. Can you explain it, Mr. Blackmore?"

"I don't think that it is very remarkable," Stephen replied. "I knew very little of my aunt's affairs, and I don't think my Uncle Jeffrey knew much more. It is not clear what money this was that she left to my uncle. She was a very taciturn woman and made few confidences to any one."

"So that it is possible," said Thorndyke, "that she, herself, may have acquired this money recently by some bequest?"

"It is quite possible," Stephen answered.

"She died, I understand," said Thorndyke, glancing at the notes that he had jotted down, "two days before Mr. Jeffrey. What date would that be?"

"Jeffrey died on the fourteenth of March," said Marchmont.

"So that Mrs. Wilson died on the twelfth of March?"

"That is so," Marchmont replied.

Thorndyke then asked, "Did she die suddenly?"

"No," replied Stephen, "she died of cancer. I understand that it was cancer of the stomach."

"Do you happen to know," Thorndyke asked, "what sort of relations existed between Jeffrey and his brother John?"

"At one time," said Stephen, "I know they were not very cordial, but the breach seems to have been made up later. I don't know that it actually was."

"I ask the question," said Thorndyke, "because, as I daresay you have noticed, there is in the first will some hint of improved relations. As it was originally drawn that will makes Mr. Stephen the sole beneficiary. Then a little later a codicil is added in favor of John, showing that Jeffrey had felt the necessity of making some recognition of the big brother. This seems to point to some change in the relations, and the question arises: if such a change did actually occur, was it the beginning of a new and further improving state of feeling between the two brothers? Have you any facts bearing on that question?"

Marchmont pursed up his lips with the air of a man considering an unwelcome suggestion, and after a few moments of reflection, answered, "I think we must say 'yes' to that. There is the undeniable fact that, of all Jeffrey's friends, John Blackmore was the only one who knew that he was living at New Inn."

"John knew that, did he?"

"Yes, he certainly did, for it came out in the evidence that he had called on Jeffrey at his chambers more than once. There is no denying that. But mark you," Mr. Marchmont added, emphatically, "that does not cover the inconsistency of the will. There is nothing in the second will to suggest that Jeffrey intended materially to increase the bequest to his brother."

"I quite agree with you, Marchmont. I think that is a perfectly sound position. You have, I suppose, fully considered the question as to whether it would be possible to set aside the second will on the ground that it fails to carry out the evident wishes and intentions of the testator?"

"Yes. My partner and I went into that question very carefully. The court would certainly uphold the will."

"I think that would be my own view," said Thorndyke, "especially after what you have told me. Did anyone else know that Jeffrey was in residence at New Inn?"

"His bankers knew and so did the officials from whom he drew his pension. And as regards the bank, I may mention that the manager tells me that of late, they had noticed a slight change in the character of Jeffrey's signature. I think you will see the reason for the change when you hear the rest of his story. It was very trifling; not more than commonly occurs when a man begins to grow old, especially if there is some failure of eyesight."

"Was Mr. Jeffrey's eyesight failing?" asked Thorndyke.

"Yes, it was, undoubtedly," said Stephen. "He was practically blind in one eye, and in the very last letter that I ever had from him, he mentioned that there were signs of a cataract in the other."

"You spoke of his pension. He continued to draw that regularly?"

"Yes; he drew his allowance every month, or rather, his bankers drew it for him. They had been accustomed to do so when he was abroad, and the authorities seem to have allowed the practice to continue."

Thorndyke reflected a while running his eye over the notes on the slips of paper in his hand, and Marchmont surveyed him with a malicious smile. Presently the latter remarked, "Methinks the learned counsel is floored."

Thorndyke laughed. "It seems to me," he retorted, "that your proceedings are rather like those of the amiable individual who offered the bear a stone, that he might crack it and extract the kernel. Your confounded will seems to offer no soft spot on which one could commence an attack, but we won't give up. Let us now have a few facts respecting the parties concerned in it; and, as Jeffrey is the central figure, let us begin with him and the tragedy at Number 31, New Inn that formed the starting point of all this trouble."

CHAPTER 6
JEFFREY BLACKMORE, DECEASED

Thorndyke placed a fresh slip of paper on the blotting pad on his knee and looked inquiringly at Mr. Marchmont, who sighed and looked at the bundle of documents on the table.

"What do you want to know?" he asked a little wearily.

"Everything," replied Thorndyke. "You have hinted at circumstances that would account for a change in Jeffrey's habits and that would explain an alteration in the character of his signature. Let us have those circumstances in which they occurred or in which they became known."

"That's the worst of you, Thorndyke," Marchmont grumbled. "When a case has been squeezed out to the last drop in a legal sense, you want to begin all over again with the family history of every one concerned and a list of his effects and household furniture. But I suppose this will have to be, and I imagine that the best way in which to give you the information you want will be to recite the circumstances surrounding the death of Jeffrey Blackmore. Will that suit you?"

"Perfectly," replied Thorndyke.

Thereupon Marchmont began. "The death of Jeffrey Blackmore was discovered at about eleven o'clock in the morning of the fifteenth of March. It seems that a builder's man was ascending a ladder to examine a gutter on New Inn. On passing a second floor window that was open at the top, he looked in and perceived a gentleman lying on a bed. The gentleman was fully clothed and had apparently lain down on the bed to rest; at least so the builder thought at the time, for he was merely passing the window on his way up, and very properly did not make a minute examination. But when some ten minutes later he came down and saw that the gentleman was still in the same position, he looked at him more attentively. This is what he noticed—but perhaps we had better have it in his own words as he told the story at the inquest.

'When I came to look at the gentleman a bit more closely, it struck me that he looked rather queer. His face looked very white, or rather pale yellow, like parchment, and his mouth was open. He did not seem to be breathing. On the bed by his side was a brass object of some kind—I could not make out what it was—and he seemed to be holding some small metal object in his hand. I thought it rather a queer affair, so when I came down I went across to the lodge and told the porter about it. The porter came out across the square with me, and I showed him the window. Then he told me to go up the stairs to Mr. Blackmore's chambers on the second floor and knock and keep on knocking until I got an answer. I went up and knocked and kept on knocking as loud as I could, but, though I fetched everybody out of all the other chambers in the house, I couldn't get any answer from Mr. Blackmore. So I went downstairs again, and then the porter sent me for a policeman.

'I went out and met a policeman just by Dane's Inn and told him about the affair, and he came back with me. He and the porter consulted together, and then they told me to go up the ladder and get in through the window and open the door of the chambers from the inside. So I went up, and as soon as I got in I saw that the gentleman was dead. I went through the other room and opened the outer door and let in the porter and the policeman.'

"That," said Mr. Marchmont, laying down the paper containing the depositions, "is the way in which poor Jeffrey Blackmore's death came to be discovered.

"The constable reported to his inspector and the inspector sent for the divisional surgeon, whom he accompanied to Number 31, New Inn. I need not go into the evidence given by the police officers, as the surgeon saw all that they saw and his statement covers everything that is known about Jeffrey's death. This is what he says, after describing how he was sent for and arrived at the Inn.

'In the bedroom, I found the body of a man between fifty and sixty years of age which has since been identified in my presence as that of Mr. Jeffrey Blackmore. It was fully dressed and wore boots on which was a moderate amount of dry mud. It was lying on its back on the bed, which did not appear to have been slept in, and showed no sign of any struggle or disturbance. The right hand loosely grasped a hypodermic syringe containing a few drops of clear liquid, which I have since analyzed and found to be a concentrated solution of toxic strophanthin.

'On the bed, close to the left side of the body was a brass opium pipe of a pattern which I believe is made in China. The bowl of the pipe contained a small quantity of charcoal and a fragment of opium together with some ash, and there was on the bed a little ash which appeared to have dropped from the bowl when the pipe fell or was laid down. On the mantelpiece in the bedroom I found a small glass jar containing about an ounce of solid opium, and another larger jar containing wood charcoal broken up into six fragments. Also a bowl containing a quantity of ash with fragments of half-burned charcoal and a few minute particles of charred opium. By the side of the bowl were a knife, a kind of awl, and a very small pair of tongs, which I believe to have been used for carrying a piece of lighted charcoal to the pipe.

'On the dressing table were two glass tubes labeled "Hypodermic Tablets: Strophanthin 1/500 grain," and a small glass mortar and pestle of which the former contained a few crystals which have since been analyzed by me and found to be this same strophanthin.

'On examining the body, I found that it had been dead about twelve hours. There were no marks of violence or any abnormal condition excepting a single puncture in the right thigh, apparently made by the needle of the hypodermic syringe.

'I made a postmortem examination of the body and found that death was due to poisoning by strophanthin, which appeared to have been injected into the thigh. The two tubes, which I found on the dressing table, would each have contained, if full, twenty tablets, each representing one five-hundredth of a grain of strophanthin. Assuming that the whole of this quantity was injected, the amount taken would be about one twelfth of a grain. The ordinary medicinal dose of strophanthin is one five-hundredth of a grain.

'I also found in the body appreciable traces of morphine—the principal alkaloid of opium—from which I infer that the deceased was a confirmed opium smoker. This inference was supported by the general condition of the body, which was ill-nourished and emaciated and presented all the appearances usually met with in the bodies of persons addicted to the habitual use of opium.'

"That is the evidence of the surgeon. He was recalled later, as we shall see, but meanwhile, I think you will agree with me that the facts testified to by him fully account, not only for the change in Jeffrey's habits—his solitary and secretive mode of life—but also for the alteration in his handwriting."

"Yes," agreed Thorndyke, "that seems to be so. By the way, what did the change in the handwriting amount to?"

"Very little," replied Marchmont. "It was hardly perceptible. Just a slight loss of firmness and distinctness; such a trifling change as you would expect to find in the handwriting of a man who had taken to anything that might impair the steadiness of his hand. I would not have noticed it myself, but of course the people at the bank are experts, constantly scrutinizing signatures with a very critical eye."

"Is there any other evidence that bears on the case?" Thorndyke asked.

Marchmont turned over the bundle of papers and smiled grimly.

"My dear Thorndyke," he said, "*none* of this evidence has the slightest bearing on the case. It is all perfectly irrelevant as far as the will is concerned. But I know your little peculiarities and I am indulging you, as you see, to the top of your bent. The next evidence is that of the chief porter, a very worthy and intelligent man named Walker. This is what he says, after the usual preliminaries.

> 'I have viewed the body, which forms the subject of this inquiry. It is that of Mr. Jeffrey Blackmore, the tenant of a set of chambers on the second floor of Number 31, New Inn. I have known the deceased nearly six months, and during that time have seen and conversed with him frequently. He took the chambers on the second of last October and came into residence at once. Tenants at New Inn have to furnish two references. The references that the deceased gave were his bankers and his brother, Mr. John Blackmore. The deceased was very well known to me. He was a quiet, pleasant-mannered gentleman, and it was his habit to drop in occasionally at the lodge and have a chat with me. I went into his chambers with him once or twice on some small matters of business, and I noticed that there were always a number of books and papers on the table.

'I understood from him that he spent most of his time indoors engaged in study and writing. I know very little about his way of living. He had no maid to look after his rooms, so I suppose he did his own housework and cooking; but he told me that he took most of his meals at restaurants or his club.

'The deceased impressed me as a rather melancholy, low-spirited gentleman. He was very much troubled about his eyesight and mentioned the matter to me on several occasions. He told me that he was practically blind in one eye and that the sight of the other was failing rapidly. He said that this afflicted him greatly, because his one pleasure in life was in the reading of books, and that if he could not read he should not wish to live. On another occasion he said that "to a blind man life was not worth living."

'On the twelfth of last November he came to the lodge with a paper in his hand which he said was his will—'

"But I needn't read that," said Marchmont, turning over the leaf, "I've told you how the will was signed and witnessed. We will pass on to the day of poor Jeffrey's death.

'On the fourteenth of March at about half past six in the evening, the deceased came to the Inn in a cab. That was the day of the great fog. I do not know if there was anyone else in the cab with the deceased, but I think not, because he came to the lodge just before eight o'clock and had a little talk with me. He said that he had been overtaken by the fog and could not see at all. He was quite blind and had been obliged to ask a stranger to call a cab for him as he could not find his way through the streets. He then gave me a check for the rent. I reminded him that the rent was not due until the twenty-fifth, but he said he wished to pay it now. He also gave me some money to pay one or two small bills that were owed—to a milkman, a baker, and a stationer.

'This struck me as very strange, because he had always managed his business and paid the trades people himself. He told me that the fog had irritated his eye so that he could hardly read, and he was afraid he should soon be quite blind. He was very depressed, so much so that I felt quite uneasy about him. When he left the lodge, he went back across the square as if returning to his chambers. There was then no gate open except for the main gate where the lodge is situated. That was the last time that I saw the deceased alive.' "

Mr. Marchmont laid the paper on the table. "That is the porter's evidence. The remaining depositions are those of Noble, the night porter, John Blackmore, and our friend here, Mr. Stephen. The night porter had not much to tell. This is the substance of his evidence.

'I have viewed the body of the deceased and identify it as that of Mr. Jeffrey Blackmore. I knew the deceased well by sight and occasionally had a few words with him. I know nothing of his habits except that he used to sit up rather late. It is one of my duties to go around the Inn at night and call out the hours until one o'clock in the morning. When calling out "one o'clock" I often saw a light in the sitting room of the deceased's chambers. On the night of the fourteenth, the light was burning until past one o'clock, but it was in the bedroom. The light in the sitting room was out by ten o'clock.'

"We now come to John Blackmore's evidence. He says:

'I have viewed the body of the deceased and recognize it as that of my brother Jeffrey. I last saw him alive on the twenty-third of February, when I called at his chambers. He then seemed in a very despondent state of mind and told me that his eyesight was fast failing. I was aware that he occasionally smoked opium, but I did not know that it was a confirmed habit. I urged him on several occasions to abandon the practice. I have no reason to believe that his affairs were in any way embarrassed or that he had any reason for despondency other than his failing eyesight.'

"That is the substance of John Blackmore's evidence, and as to Mr. Stephen, his statement merely sets forth the fact that he had identified the body as that of his Uncle Jeffrey. And now I think you have all the facts. Is there anything more that you want to ask me before I go? I must really run away now."

"I should like," said Thorndyke, "to know a little more about the parties concerned in this affair. But perhaps Mr. Stephen can give me the information."

"I expect he can," said Marchmont. "At any rate, he knows more about them than I do, so I will be off. If you should happen to think of any way," he continued with a sly smile, "of upsetting that will, just let me know, and I will lose no time in entering a caveat. Goodbye. Don't trouble to let me out."

As soon as he was gone, Thorndyke turned to Stephen Blackmore. "I am going to ask you a few questions which may appear rather trifling, but you must remember that my methods of inquiry concern themselves with persons and things rather than with documents. For instance, I have not gathered very completely what sort of person your Uncle Jeffrey was. Could you tell me a little more about him?"

"What shall I tell you?" Stephen asked with a slightly embarrassed air.

"Well, begin with his personal appearance."

"That is rather difficult to describe." said Stephen. "He was a medium-sized man and about five feet seven, fair, slightly gray, clean shaven, rather spare and slight, had gray eyes, wore spectacles, and stooped a little as he walked. He was quiet and gentle in manner, rather yielding and irresolute in character, and his health was not at all robust though he had no infirmity or disease excepting his bad eyesight. His age was about fifty-five."

"How came he to be on disability at fifty-five?" asked Thorndyke.

"Oh, that was through an accident. He had a nasty fall from a horse. It seems that the fall damaged his eyes in some way; in fact he practically lost the sight of one—the right—from that moment; and as that had been his good eye, the accident left his vision very much impaired. So he was at first given sick leave and then allowed to retire on a pension."

Thorndyke noted these particulars and then said, "Your uncle has been more than once referred to as a man of studious habits. Does that mean that he pursued any particular branch of learning?"

"Yes. He was an enthusiastic Oriental scholar. His official duties had taken him at one time to Tokyo and at another to Baghdad, and while at those places he gave a good deal of attention to the languages, literature, and arts of the countries. He was also greatly interested in Babylonian and Assyrian archeology, and I believe he assisted for some time in the excavations at Birs Nimroud."

"Indeed!" said Thorndyke. "This is very interesting. I had no idea that he was a man of such considerable attainments. The facts mentioned by Mr. Marchmont would hardly have led one to think of him as what he seems to have been— a scholar of some distinction."

"I don't know that Mr. Marchmont realized the fact himself," said Stephen, "or that he would have considered it of any importance if he had."

"You can never tell beforehand," said Thorndyke, "what facts may turn out to be of consequence, so that it is best to collect all you can get. By the way, were you aware that your uncle was an opium smoker?"

"No, I was not. I knew that he had a pipe which he brought with him when he came home from Japan, but I thought it was only a curio. I remember him telling me that he once tried a few puffs at an opium pipe and found that it gave him a headache, but I had no idea he had contracted the habit. In fact, I may say that I was utterly astonished when the fact came out at the inquest."

Thorndyke made a note of this answer too, and said, "I think that is all I have to ask you about your Uncle Jeffrey. And now as to Mr. John Blackmore. What sort of man is he?"

"I am afraid I can't tell you very much about him. Until I saw him at the inquest, I had not seen him since I was a boy. But he is a very different kind of man from Uncle Jeffrey, different in appearance and different in character."

"You would say that the two brothers were physically quite unlike then?"

"Well," said Stephen, "I don't know that I ought to say that. Perhaps I am exaggerating the difference. I am thinking of Uncle Jeffrey as he was when I saw him last and of Uncle John as he appeared at the inquest. They were very different then. Jeffrey was thin, pale, clean-shaven, wore spectacles, and walked with a stoop. John is a shade taller, a shade grayer, has good eyesight, a healthy, florid complexion, a brisk, upright carriage, is distinctly stout, and wears a beard and moustache which are black and only very slightly streaked with gray. To me they looked as unlike as two men could, though their features were really of the same type. Indeed, I have heard it said that as young men, they were rather alike, and they both resembled their mother. But there is no doubt as to their difference in character. Jeffrey was quiet, serious, and studious, whereas John rather inclined to frequent races, and I think gambled a good deal at times."

"What is his profession?"

"That would be difficult to tell; he has so many; he is so very versatile. I believe he began life as an assistant in the laboratory of a large brewery, but he soon left that and went on the stage. He seems to have remained in that profession for some years, touring about this country and making occasional visits to America. The life seemed to suit him, and I believe he was decidedly successful as an actor. But suddenly he left the stage and blossomed out in connection with a bucket shop—a fraudulent brokerage—in London."

"And what is he doing now?"

"At the inquest he described himself as a stockbroker, so I presume he is still connected with the bucket shop."

Thorndyke rose and taking down from the reference shelves a list of members of the stock exchange, turned over the leaves.

"Yes," he said, replacing the volume, "he must be an outside broker. His name is not in the list of members of 'the House.' From what you tell me, it is easy to understand that there should have been no great intimacy between the two brothers, without assuming any kind of ill feeling. They simply had very little in common. Anything more?"

"No. I have never heard of any actual quarrel or disagreement. My impression that they did not get on very well may have been due to the terms of the will, especially the first will. And they certainly did not seek one another's company."

"That is not very conclusive," said Thorndyke. "As to the will, a thrifty man is not usually much inclined to bequeath big savings to a gentleman who may probably employ them in a merry little flutter on the race track or the stock exchange. And then there was yourself, clearly a more suitable subject for a legacy, as your life is all before you. But this is mere speculation, and the matter is not of much importance, as far as we can see. And now, tell me what John Blackmore's relations were with Mrs. Wilson. I gather that she left the bulk of her property to Jeffrey, her younger brother. Is that so?"

"Yes. She left nothing to John. The fact is that they were hardly on speaking terms. I believe John had treated her rather badly, or at any rate she thought he had. Mr. Wilson, her late husband, had lost some money over an investment in connection with the brokerage that I spoke of."

"Did you know your aunt well?"

"No; very slightly. She lived down in Devonshire and saw very little of any of us. She was a taciturn, strong-minded woman; quite unlike her brothers. She seems to have resembled her father's family."

"You might give me her full name."

"Julia Elizabeth Wilson. Her husband's name was Edmund Wilson."

"Thank you. There is just one more point. What has happened to your uncle's chambers in New Inn since his death?"

"They have remained shut up. As all his effects were left to me, I have taken over the tenancy for the present to avoid having them disturbed. I thought of keeping them for my own use, but I don't think I could live there after what I have seen."

"You have inspected them then?"

"Yes; I have just looked through them. I went there on the day of the inquest."

"Tell me. As you looked through those rooms, what kind of impression did they convey to you as to your uncle's habits and mode of life?"

Stephen smiled apologetically. "I am afraid," said he, "that they did not convey any particular impression in that respect. I looked into the sitting room and saw all his old familiar household goods, and then I went into the bedroom and saw the impression on the bed where his corpse had lain, and that gave me such a sensation of horror that I came away at once."

"But the appearance of the rooms must have conveyed something to your mind," Thorndyke urged.

"I am afraid it did not. You see, I have not your analytical eye. But perhaps you would like to look through them yourself? If you would, pray do so. They are my chambers now."

"I think I should like to glance around them," Thorndyke replied.

"Very well," said Stephen. "I will give you my calling card now, and I will look in at the lodge presently and tell the porter to hand you the key whenever you like to look over the rooms."

He took a card from his case, and having written a few lines on it, handed it to Thorndyke.

"It is very good of you," he said, "to take so much trouble. Like Mr. Marchmont, I have no expectation of any result from your efforts, but I am very grateful to you, all the same, for going into the case so thoroughly. I suppose you don't see any possibility of upsetting that will, if I may ask the question?"

"At present," replied Thorndyke, "I do not. But until I have carefully weighed every fact connected with the case—whether it seems to have any bearing or not—I shall refrain from expressing, or even entertaining, an opinion either way."

Stephen Blackmore now took his leave, and Thorndyke, having collected the papers containing his notes, neatly punched a couple of holes in their margins and inserted them into a small notebook, which he slipped into his pocket.

"That," said he, "is the nucleus of the body of data on which our investigations must be based, and I very much fear that it will not receive any great additions. What do you think, Jervis?"

"The case looks about as hopeless as a case could look," I replied.

"That is what I think," said he, "and for that reason I am more than ordinarily keen on making something of it. I have not much more hope than Marchmont has, but I shall squeeze the case as dry as a bone before I let it go. What are you going to do?"

"Shall I walk down with you?"

"It is very good of you to offer, Jervis, but I think I will go on alone. I want to run over these notes and get the facts of the case arranged in my mind. Knowledge is of no use unless it is actually in your mind, so that it can be produced at a moment's notice. So you had better get a book and spend a quiet hour by the fire while I assimilate the miscellaneous mental feast that we have just enjoyed. And you might do a little rumination yourself."

With this Thorndyke took his departure, and I adopting his advice drew my chair closer to the fire. But I did not discover any inclination to read. The curious history that I had just heard, and Thorndyke's evident determination to examine it further, disposed me to meditation. Moreover, as his subordinate, it was my business to occupy myself with his affairs. Wherefore, having stirred the fire, I abandoned myself to the renewed consideration of the facts relating to Jeffrey Blackmore's will.

CHAPTER 7
THE CUNEIFORM INSCRIPTION

The surprise which Thorndyke's proceedings usually occasioned, especially to lawyers, was principally due, I think, to my friend's habit of viewing occurrences from an unusual standpoint. He did not look at things quite as other men looked at them. He had no prejudices, and he knew no conventions. When other men were cocksure, Thorndyke was doubtful. When other men despaired, he entertained hopes, and thus it happened that he would often undertake cases that had been rejected contemptuously by experienced lawyers, and what is more, would bring them to a successful conclusion.

Was it conceivable that he could make anything of the present case? He had not declined it. He had certainly entertained it and was probably thinking it over at this moment. Yet could anything be more impossible? Here was the case of a man making his own will, probably writing it out himself, bringing it voluntarily to a certain place, and executing it in the presence of competent witnesses. There was no suggestion of any compulsion, influence, or persuasion. The testator was admittedly sane and responsible; and if the will did not give effect to his wishes—which could not be proved—that was due to his own carelessness in drafting the will and not to any unusual circumstances. And so the problem was how to set aside that will.

I reviewed the statements that I had heard, but turn them about as I would, I could get nothing out of them but confirmation of Mr. Marchmont's estimate of the case. One fact that I had noted with some curiosity I again considered; that was Thorndyke's evident desire to inspect Jeffrey Blackmore's chambers. He had shown no eagerness, but I had seen at the time that the questions, which he put to Stephen, were put not with any expectation of eliciting information but for the purpose of getting an opportunity to look over the rooms himself.

I was still cogitating on the subject when my colleague returned, followed by the watchful Polton with the tea tray, and I attacked him forthwith.

"Well, Thorndyke," I said, "I have been thinking about this Blackmore case while you have been gadding about."

"And may I take it that the problem is solved?"

"No. I can make nothing of it."

"Then you are in much the same position as I am."

"But if you can make nothing of it, why did you undertake it?"

"I only undertook to think about it," said Thorndyke. "I never reject a case out of hand unless it is obviously fishy. It is surprising how difficulties, and even impossibilities, dwindle if you look at them attentively. My experience has taught me that the most unlikely case is at least worth thinking over."

"Why do you want to look over Jeffrey's chambers? What do you expect to find there?"

"I have no expectations at all. I am simply looking for stray facts."

"And all those questions that you asked Stephen Blackmore; had you nothing in your mind, no definite purpose?"

"No purpose beyond getting to know as much about the case as I can."

"But," I exclaimed, "do you mean that you are going to examine those rooms without any definite object at all?"

"I wouldn't say that," replied Thorndyke. "This is a legal case. Let me put an analogous medical case before you. Supposing that a man should consult you about a progressive loss of weight. He can give no explanation. He has no pain, no discomfort, no symptoms of any kind. In short, he feels perfectly well in every respect, but he is losing weight continuously. What would you do?"

"I should overhaul him thoroughly," I answered.

"Why? What would you expect to find?"

"I don't know that I should start by expecting to find anything in particular. But I should overhaul him organ by organ and function by function, and if I could find nothing abnormal, I should have to give it up."

"Exactly," said Thorndyke. "And that is just my position and my line of action. Here is a case which is perfectly regular and straightforward excepting in one respect. It has a single abnormal feature. And for that abnormality there is nothing to account.

"Jeffrey Blackmore made a will. It was a well drawn will, and it apparently gave full effect to his intentions. Then he revoked that will and made another. No change had occurred in his circumstances or in his intentions. The provisions of the new will were believed by him to be identical with those of the old one. The new will differed from the old one only in having a defect in the drafting from which the first will was free, and of which he must have been unaware. Now why did he revoke the first will and replace it with another which he believed to be identical in its provisions? There is no answer to that question. It is an abnormal feature in the case. There must be some explanation of that abnormality, and it is my business to discover it. But the facts in my possession yield no such explanation. Therefore it is my purpose to search for new facts which may give me a starting point for an investigation."

This exposition of Thorndyke's proposed conduct of the case, reasonable as it was, did not impress me as very convincing. I found myself coming back to Marchmont's position, that there was really nothing to dispute. But other matters claimed our attention at the moment, and it was not until after dinner that my colleague returned to the subject.

"How would you like to take a turn around to New Inn this evening?" he asked.

"I should have thought," said I, "that it would be better to go by daylight. Those old chambers are not usually very well illuminated."

"Good thought," said Thorndyke. "We had better take a lamp with us. Let us go up to the laboratory and get one from Polton."

"There is no need to do that," said I. "The pocket lamp that you lent me is in my overcoat pocket. I put it there to return it to you."

"Did you have occasion to use it?" he asked.

"Yes. I paid another visit to the mysterious house and carried out your plan. I must tell you about it later."

"Do. I shall be keenly interested to hear all about your adventures. Is there plenty of candle left in the lamp?"

"Oh yes. I only used it for about an hour."

"Then let us be off," said Thorndyke, and we accordingly set forth on our quest.

"I can't imagine," said I, "that you have absolutely nothing in view. That you are going to this place with no defined purpose whatever."

"I did not say exactly that," replied Thorndyke. "I said that I was not going to look for any particular thing or fact. I am going in the hope that I may observe something that may start a new train of speculation. But that is not all. You know that an investigation follows a certain logical course. It begins with the observation of the conspicuous facts. We have done that. The facts were supplied by Marchmont. The next stage is to propose to oneself one or more provisional explanations or hypotheses. We have done that too—or at least I have, and I suppose you have."

"I haven't," I said. "But I should like to hear your theories on the subject."

"You won't hear them at present. They are mere wild conjectures. But to resume: what do we do next?"

"Go to New Inn and rake over the deceased gentleman's apartments?"

Thorndyke smilingly ignored my answer and continued, "We examine each explanation in turn and see what follows from it; whether it agrees with all the facts and leads to the discovery of new ones, or on the other hand, disagrees with some facts or leads us to an absurdity.

"So we proceed in cases like this present one. Of the facts that are known to us, we invent certain explanations. From each of those explanations we deduce consequences; and if those consequences agree with new facts, they confirm the explanation, whereas if they disagree, they tend to disprove it. But here we are at our destination."

We turned out of Wych Street into the arched passage leading into New Inn and, halting at the half door of the lodge, perceived a stout, purple-faced man crouching over the fire, coughing violently. He held up his hand to intimate that he was fully occupied for the moment, and we accordingly waited for his paroxysm to subside. At length he turned towards us, wiping his eyes, and inquired our business.

"Mr. Stephen Blackmore," said Thorndyke, "has given me permission to look over his chambers. He said that he would mention the matter to you."

"So he has, sir," said the porter, "but he has just taken the key himself to go to the chambers. You'll find him there. It's on the far side—Number 31, second floor."

We made our way across to the house indicated, the ground floor of which was occupied by offices and was distinguished by a good-sized brass plate. Although it had now been dark some time, there was no light on the lower stairs, but we encountered on the first floor landing a man who had just lit the lamp there. Thorndyke halted to address him.

"Can you tell me who occupies the chambers on the third floor?"

"The third floor has been empty about three months," was the reply.

"We are going up to look at the chambers on the second floor," said Thorndyke. "Are they pretty quiet?"

"Quiet!" exclaimed the man. "Why, the place is like a cemetery for the deaf and dumb. There's the solicitors on the ground floor and the architects on the first floor. They both clear out about six, and when they're gone, the 'ouse is as empty as a blown hegg. I don't wonder poor Mr. Blackmore made away with hisself. Livin' up there all alone, it must have been like Robinson Crusoe without no man Friday and not even a blooming goat to talk to. Quiet! It's quiet enough, if that's what you want. Wouldn't be no good to me."

With a contemptuous shake of the head, he turned and retired down the next flight, and as the echoes of his footsteps died away, we resumed our ascent.

"So it would appear," Thorndyke commented, "that when Jeffrey Blackmore came home that last evening, the house was empty."

Arriving on the second floor landing, we were confronted by a solid looking door on the lintel of which the deceased man's name was painted in white lettering, which still looked new and fresh. Thorndyke knocked at the door, which was at once opened by Stephen Blackmore.

"I haven't wasted any time before taking advantage of your permission, you see," my colleague said as we entered.

"No, indeed," said Stephen. "You are very prompt. I have been rather wondering what kind of information you expect to gather from an inspection of these rooms."

Thorndyke smiled genially, amused no doubt by the similarity of Stephen's remarks to those of mine which he had so recently criticized.

"A man of science, Mr. Blackmore," he said, "expects nothing. He collects facts and keeps an open mind. As for me, I am a snapper-up of unconsidered trifles of evidence. When I have accumulated a few facts, I arrange them, compare them, and think about them. Sometimes the comparison yields new matter and sometimes it doesn't; but in any case, believe me, it is a capital error to decide beforehand what facts are to be sought."

"Yes, I suppose that is so," said Stephen, "though to me it almost looks as if Mr. Marchmont was right, that there is nothing to investigate."

"You should have thought of that before you consulted me," laughed Thorndyke. "As it is, I am engaged to look into the case, and I shall do so. As I have said, I shall keep an open mind until I have all the facts in my possession."

He glanced around the sitting room, which we had now entered, and continued, "These are fine, dignified old rooms. It seems a sin to have covered up all this oak-paneling and that carved cornice and mantel with paint. Think what it must have been like when the beautiful figured wood was exposed."

"It would be very dark," Stephen observed.

"Yes," Thorndyke agreed, "and I suppose we care more for light and less for beauty than our ancestors did. But now, tell me; looking around these rooms, do they convey to you a similar impression to that which his old rooms did? Have they the same general character?"

"Not quite, I think. Of course the rooms in Jermyn Street were in a different kind of house, but beyond that, I seem to feel a certain difference, which is rather odd, seeing that the furniture is the same. But the old rooms were more cozy, more homelike. I find something rather bare and cheerless—I was almost going to say squalid—in the look of these chambers."

"That is rather what I should have expected," said Thorndyke. "The opium habit alters a man's character profoundly, and somehow, apart from the mere furnishing, a room reflects in some subtle way, but very distinctly, the personality of its occupant, especially when that occupant lives a solitary life. Do you see any evidences of the activities that used to occupy your uncle?"

"Not much," replied Stephen. "But the place may not be quite as he left it. I found one or two of his books on the table and put them back in the shelves, but I found no manuscript or notes such as he used to make. I noticed, too, that his ink slab, which he used to keep so scrupulously clean, is covered with dry smears and that the stick of ink is all cracked at the end, as if he had not used it for months. It seems to point to a great change in his habits."

"What did he do with Chinese ink?" Thorndyke asked.

"He corresponded with some of his native friends in Japan. He used to write in the Japanese character even if they understood English. That was what he chiefly used the Chinese ink for, but he also used to copy the inscriptions from these things." Here Stephen lifted from the mantelpiece what looked like a fossil but was actually a clay tablet covered with minute indented writing.

"Your uncle could read the cuneiform character then?"

"Yes; he was something of an expert. These tablets are, I believe, leases and other legal documents from Eridu and other Babylonian cities. He used to copy the inscriptions in the cuneiform writing and then translate them into English. But I mustn't stay here any longer as I have an engagement for this evening. I just dropped in to get these two volumes— Thornton's *History of Babylonia*—which he once advised me to read. Shall I give you the key? You'd better have it and leave it with the porter as you go out."

He shook hands with us, and we walked out with him to the landing and stood watching him as he ran down the stairs. Glancing at Thorndyke by the light of the gas lamp on the landing, I thought I detected in his impassive face that almost imperceptible change of expression to which I have already alluded as indicating pleasure or satisfaction.

"You are looking quite pleased with yourself," I remarked.

"I am not displeased," he replied calmly. "I have picked up a few crumbs—very small ones, but still crumbs. No doubt my learned junior has picked up a few likewise?"

I shook my head . . . and inwardly suspected it of being rather a thick head.

"I did not perceive anything in the least degree significant in what Stephen was telling you," I said. "It was all very interesting, but it did not seem to have any bearing on his uncle's will."

"I was not referring only to what Stephen has told us, although that was, as you say, very interesting. While he was talking, I was looking about the room, and I have seen a very strange thing. Let me show it to you."

He linked his arm in mine and walking me back into the room, halted opposite the fireplace.

"There," said he, "look at that. It is a most remarkable object."

I followed the direction of his gaze and saw an oblong frame enclosing a large photograph of an inscription in a weird arrowhead character. I looked at it in silence for some seconds and then, somewhat disappointed, remarked, "I don't see anything very remarkable in it under the circumstances. In any ordinary room it would be, I admit, but Stephen has just told us that his uncle was something of an expert in cuneiform writing."

"Exactly," said Thorndyke. "That is my point. That is what makes it so remarkable."

"I don't follow you at all," said I. "That a man should hang upon his wall an inscription that is legible to him does not seem to me at all out of the way. It would be much more singular if he should hang up an inscription that he could not read."

"No doubt," replied Thorndyke. "But you will agree with me that it would be still more singular if a man should hang upon his wall an inscription that he could read . . . and hang it upside down."

I stared at Thorndyke in amazement.

"Do you mean to tell me," I exclaimed, "that that photograph is really upside down?"

"I do indeed," he replied.

"But how do you know? Are you yet another Oriental scholar?"

Thorndyke chuckled. "Some fool," he replied, "has said that 'a little knowledge is a dangerous thing.' Compared with much knowledge, it may be, but it is a vast deal better than no knowledge. Here is a case in point. I have read with very keen interest the wonderful history of the decipherment of the cuneiform writing, and I happen to recollect one or two of the main facts that seemed to me to be worth remembering. Now this script consists, as you see, of two kinds of characters:

the small, solid, acutely pointed characters, which are known as wedges, and the larger, more obtuse characters, called arrowheads. The names are rather unfortunate, as both forms are wedge like and both resemble arrowheads. The script reads from left to right, like our own writing, and the rule for the placing of the characters is that all the wedges point to the right or downwards, and the arrowhead forms are open towards the right. But if you look at this photograph, you will see that all the wedges point upwards to the left and that the arrowhead characters are open towards the left. Obviously the photograph is upside down."

"But," I exclaimed, "this is really most mysterious. What do you suppose can be the explanation?"

"I think," replied Thorndyke, "that we may perhaps get a suggestion from the back of the frame. Let us see."

He disengaged the frame from the two nails on which it hung, and turning it around, glanced at the back, which he then presented for my inspection. A label on the backing paper bore the words, "J. Budge, Framemaker and Gilder, 16, Gt. Anne Street, W.C."

"Well?" I said, when I had read the label without gathering from it anything fresh.

"The label, you observe, is the right way up as it hangs on the wall."

"So it is," I rejoined hastily, a little annoyed that I had not been quicker to observe so obvious a fact. "I see your point. You mean that the frame maker hung the thing upside down, and Jeffrey never noticed the mistake?"

"That is a perfectly sound explanation," said Thorndyke. "But I think there is something more. You will notice that the label is an old one; it must have been on some years to judge by its dingy appearance, whereas the two plates look to me comparatively new. But we can soon put that matter to the test, for the label was evidently stuck on when the frame was new, and if the plates were screwed on at the same time, the wood that they cover will be clean and new looking."

He drew from his pocket a knife containing, among other implements, a screwdriver with which he carefully extracted the screws from one of the little brass plates by which the frame had been suspended from the nails.

"You see," he said, when he had removed the plate and carried the photograph over to the gas jet, "the wood covered by the plate is as dirty and time stained as the rest of the frame. The plates have been put on recently."

"And what are we to infer from that?"

"Well, since there are no other marks of plates or rings upon the frame, we may safely infer that the photograph was never hung up until it came to these rooms."

"Yes, I suppose we may. But what then? What inference does that lead to?"

Thorndyke reflected for a few moments, and so I continued, "It is evident that this photograph suggests more to you than it does to me. I should like to hear your exposition of its bearing on the case, if it has any."

"Whether or not it has any real bearing on the case," Thorndyke answered, "it is impossible for me to say at this stage. I told you that I had proposed to myself one or two hypotheses to account for and explain Jeffrey Blackmore's will, and I will say that the curious misplacement of this photograph fits more than one of them. I won't say more than that, because I think it would be profitable for you to work at this case independently. You have all the facts that I have, and you shall have a copy of my notes of Marchmont's statement of the case. With this material you ought to be able to reach some conclusion. Of course neither of us may be able to make anything of the case. It doesn't look very hopeful at present. But whatever happens, we can compare notes after the event, and you will be the richer by so much experience of actual investigation. But I will start you off with one hint, which is this:

The Cuneiform Inscription

neither you nor Marchmont seem to appreciate in the least the very extraordinary nature of the facts that he communicated to us."

"I thought Marchmont seemed pretty much alive to the fact that it was a very queer will."

"So he did," agreed Thorndyke. "But that is not quite what I mean. The whole set of circumstances taken together and in relation to one another impressed me as most remarkable, and that is why I'm giving so much attention to what looks at first sight like such a very unpromising case. Copy out my notes, Jervis, and examine the facts critically. I think you will see what I mean. And now let us proceed."

He replaced the brass plate and having reinserted the screws, hung up the frame, and proceeded to browse slowly around the room, stopping now and again to inspect the Japanese prints and framed photographs of buildings and other objects of archeological interest that formed the only attempts at wall decoration. To one of the former he drew my attention.

"These things are of some value," he remarked.

"Here is one by Utamaro—that little circle with the mark over it is his signature—and you notice that the paper is becoming spotted in places with mildew. The fact is worth noting in more than one connection."

I accordingly made a mental note, and the walk continued.

"You observe that Jeffrey used a gas stove, instead of a coal fire, no doubt to economize, but perhaps for other reasons. Presumably he cooked by gas too. Let us see."

We wandered into the little cupboard-like kitchen and glanced round. A ring burner on a shelf, a kettle, a frying pan, and a few pieces of crockery were its sole appointments. Apparently the porter was correct in his statement as to Jeffrey's habits.

Returning to the sitting room, Thorndyke resumed his inspection, pulling out drawers, peering inquisitively into cupboards, and bestowing a passing glance on each of the comparatively few objects that the comfortless room contained.

"I have never seen a more characterless apartment," was his final comment. "There is nothing that seems to suggest any kind of habitual activity on the part of the occupant. Let us look at the bedroom."

We passed into the chamber of tragic memories, and when Thorndyke had lit the gas, we stood awhile looking about us in silence. It was a bare, comfortless room, dirty, neglected, and squalid. The bed appeared not to have been remade since the catastrophe.

"Well," Thorndyke remarked at length, "there is character enough here—of a kind. Jeffrey Blackmore would seem to have been a man of few needs."

He looked about him keenly and continued, "The syringe and the rest of the lethal appliances and material have been taken away, I see. Probably the analyst did not return them. But there are the opium pipe and the jar and the ash bowl, and I presume those are the clothes that the undertakers removed from the body. Shall we look them over?"

He took up the clothes, which lay, roughly folded, on a chair, and held them up, garment by garment.

"These are evidently the trousers," he remarked, spreading them out on the bed. "Here is a little white spot on the middle of the thigh which looks like a patch of small crystals from a drop of the solution. Just light the lamp, Jervis, and let us examine it with a lens."

I lit the lamp, and when we had examined the spot minutely and identified it as a mass of minute crystals, Thorndyke asked, "What do you make of those creases? You see there is one on each leg."

"It looks as if the trousers had been turned up. But if they have been, they must have been turned up about seven inches.

Poor Jeffrey couldn't have had much regard for appearances, for they would have been right above his socks. But perhaps the creases were made in undressing the body."

"That is possible," said Thorndyke, "though I don't quite see how it would have happened. I notice that his pockets seem to have been emptied. No, wait. Here is something in the waistcoat pocket."

He drew out a shabby card case and a stump of lead pencil. He looked at the latter with what seemed to me much more interest than was deserved by so commonplace an object.

"The cards, you observe," said he, "are printed from type, not from a plate. I would note that fact. And tell me what you make of that."

He handed me the pencil, which I examined with concentrated attention, helping myself even with the lamp and my pocket lens. But even with these aids I failed to discover anything unusual in its appearance. Thorndyke watched me with a mischievous smile and when I had finished, inquired, "Well, what is it?"

"Confound you!" I exclaimed. "It's a pencil. Any fool can see that, and this particular fool can't see any more. It's a wretched stump of a pencil, horribly cut to an abominably bad point. It is colored dark red on the outside and was stamped with some name that began with *C-O* . . . Cooperative Stores, perhaps."

"Now, my dear Jervis," Thorndyke protested, "don't begin by confusing speculation with fact. The letters which remain are *C-O*. Note that fact and find out what pencils there are which have inscriptions beginning with those letters. I am not going to help you, because you can easily do this for yourself. And it will be good discipline even if the fact turns out to mean nothing."

At this moment he stepped back suddenly and looking down at the floor, said, "Give me the lamp, Jervis. I've stepped on something that felt like glass."

I brought the lamp to the place where he had been standing close by the bed, and we both knelt on the floor, throwing the light of the lamp on the bare and dusty boards. Under the bed, just within reach of the foot of a person standing close by was a little patch of glass fragments. Thorndyke produced a piece of paper from his pocket and delicately swept the little fragments on to it remarking, "By the look of things, I am not the first person who has trodden on that object, whatever it is. Do you mind holding the lamp while I inspect the remains?"

I took the lamp and held it over the paper while he examined the little heap of glass through his lens.

"Well," I asked, "What have you found?"

"That is what I am asking myself," he replied. "As far as I can judge by the appearance of these fragments, they appear to be portions of a small watch glass. I wish there were some larger pieces."

"Perhaps there are," said I. "Let us look about the floor under the bed."

We resumed our groping about the dirty floor, throwing the light of the lamp on one spot after another. Presently, as we moved the lamp about, the light fell on a small glass bead, which I instantly picked up and exhibited to Thorndyke.

"Is this of any interest to you?" I asked.

Thorndyke took the bead and examined it curiously.

"It is certainly," he said, "a very odd thing to find in the bedroom of an old bachelor like Jeffrey, especially as we know that he employed no woman to look after his rooms. Of course, it may be a relic of the last tenant. Let us see if there are any more."

We renewed our search, crawling under the bed and throwing the light of the lamp in all directions over the floor.

The result was the discovery of three more beads, one entire tubular bead and the crushed remains of another. All of these, including the fragments of the bead that had been crushed, Thorndyke placed carefully on the paper which he laid on the dressing table the more conveniently to examine our find.

"I am sorry," said he, "that there are no more fragments of the watch glass, or whatever it was. The broken pieces were evidently picked up with the exception of the one that I trod on, which was obviously overlooked. As to the beads, they must have been dropped during Jeffrey's tenancy and probably quite recently."

"What sort of garment do you suppose they came from?" I asked.

"They may have been part of a beaded veil or the trimming of a dress, but the grouping rather suggests to me a piece of beaded fringe. The color is rather unusual."

"I thought they looked like black beads."

"So they do by this light, but I think that by daylight we shall find them to be a dark, reddish brown. You can see the color now if you look at the smaller fragments of the one that is crushed."

He handed me his lens, and when I had verified his statement, he produced from his pocket a small tin box with a lid in which he deposited the paper, having first folded it up into a small parcel.

"We will put the pencil in too," said he, and as he returned the box to his pocket, he added, "you had better get one of these little boxes from Polton. It is often useful to have a safe receptacle for small and fragile articles."

He folded up and replaced the dead man's clothes as we had found them. Then observing a pair of shoes standing by the wall, he picked them up and looked them over thoughtfully, paying special attention to the backs of the soles and the fronts of the heels.

"I suppose we may take it," said he, "that these are the shoes that poor Jeffrey wore on the night of his death. At any rate, there seem to be no others. He seems to have been a fairly clean walker. The streets were shockingly dirty that day, as I remember most distinctly. Do you see any slippers? I haven't noticed any."

He opened and peeped into a cupboard in which hung an overcoat surmounted by a felt hat. He looked in all the corners and into the sitting room, but no slippers were to be seen.

"Our friend seems to have had surprisingly little regard for comfort," Thorndyke remarked. "Think of spending the winter evenings in damp boots by a gas fire!"

"Perhaps he may have gone to bed early."

"But he did not. The night porter used to see the light in his rooms at one o'clock in the morning. In the sitting room too, you remember. But he seems to have been in the habit of reading in bed, for here is a candlestick with the remains of a whole dynasty of candles in it.

"He seems to have had a fair amount of clothing," said Thorndyke, who was now going through the chest of drawers, "though the shirts have a rather yellow and faded appearance. I wonder how he managed about his washing. Why, here are a couple of pairs of boots in the drawer with his clothes! And here is his stock of candles. Quite a large box . . . though nearly empty now."

He closed the drawer and cast another inquiring look around the room.

"I think we have seen all now, Jervis," he said, "unless there is anything more that you would like to look into?"

"No," I replied. "I have seen all that I wanted to see and more than I am able to attach any meaning to. So we may as well go."

I blew out the lamp and put it in my overcoat pocket, and when we had turned out the gas in both rooms, we took our departure.

As we approached the lodge, we found our stout friend in the act of retiring in favor of the night porter. Thorndyke handed him the key of the chambers, and after a few sympathetic inquiries about his health, said, "Let me see, you were one of the witnesses to Mr. Blackmore's will, I think?"

"I was, sir," replied the porter.

"And I believe you read the document through before you witnessed the signature."

"I did, sir."

"Did you read it aloud?"

"Aloud, sir? Mercy, bless you, no, sir! Why should I? The other witness read it, and of course, Mr. Blackmore knew what was in it, seeing that it was in his own handwriting. What should I want to read it aloud for?"

"No, of course you wouldn't want to. By the way, I have been wondering how Mr. Blackmore managed about his washing."

The porter evidently regarded this question with some disfavor, for he replied only with an interrogative grunt. It was, in fact, rather an odd question.

"Did you get it done for him?" Thorndyke pursued.

"No, certainly not, sir. He got it done for himself. The laundry people used to deliver the basket here at the lodge, and Mr. Blackmore used to take it in with him when he happened to be passing."

"It was not delivered to his chambers then?"

"No, sir. Mr. Blackmore was a very studious gentleman, and he didn't like to be disturbed."

Thorndyke cordially bid the porter good night, and we passed through the gateway into Wych Street. Then turning our faces eastward towards the Temple, we set forth in silence, each thinking his own thoughts. What Thorndyke's were I cannot tell, though I have no doubt that he was busily engaged in piecing together all that he had seen and heard and considering its possible application to the case in hand.

As for me, my mind was in a whirl of confusion. All this searching and examining seemed to be the mere flogging of a dead horse. The will was obviously a perfectly valid and regular will, and that was the end of the matter. At least, so it seemed to me. But that was not Thorndyke's view. His investigations were certainly not purposeless, and as I walked by his side trying to conceive some purpose in his actions, I only became more and more mystified as I recalled them one by one. Perhaps most curious of all were the cryptic questions that I had just heard him pose to the equally mystified porter.

CHAPTER 8
THE TRACK CHART

As Thorndyke and I arrived at the main gateway of the Temple and he swung round into the narrow lane, I suddenly realized that I had made no arrangements for the night. Events had followed one another so continuously and each had been so engrossing that I had lost sight of what I may call my domestic affairs.

"We seem to be heading for your chambers, Thorndyke," I ventured to remark. "It is a little late to think of it, but I have not yet settled where I am to put up tonight."

"My dear fellow," he replied, "you are going to put up in your own bedroom which has been waiting in readiness for you ever since you left it. Polton went up and inspected it as soon as you arrived."

"That is very handsome of you," said I. "You didn't mention that the lodging you offered was a resident appointment."

"Room and board included," said Thorndyke, and when I protested that I should at least contribute to the cost of living, he impatiently waved the suggestion away. We were still arguing the question when we reached our chambers—as I will now call them—and a diversion was occasioned by my taking the lamp from my pocket and placing it on the table.

"Ah," my colleague remarked, "that is a little reminder. We will put it on the mantelpiece for Polton to collect, and you shall give me a full account of your further adventures in the wilds of Kennington. That was a very odd affair. I have often wondered how it ended."

He drew our two armchairs up to the fire, put on some more coal, and settled himself with the air of a man who is anticipating an agreeable conversation.

I took up the thread of the story where I had broken off on the last occasion and began to outline my later experiences. But he brought me up short.

"Don't be sketchy, Jervis. To be sketchy is to be vague. Detail, my child, detail is the soul of induction. Let us have all the facts. We can sort them out afterwards."

I began anew in a vein of extreme detail. With deliberate malice I loaded a tedious narrative with every triviality that a fairly retentive memory could rake out of the half-forgotten past. I cudgeled my brains for irrelevant incidents. I described with the minutest accuracy things that had not the faintest significance. I drew a vivid picture of the carriage inside and out; I painted a lifelike portrait of the horse, even going into particulars of the harness—which I was surprised to find that I had noticed. I described the furniture of the dining room and the cobwebs that had hung from the ceiling; the auction ticket on the chest of drawers, the rickety table and the melancholy chairs. I gave the number per minute of the patient's respirations and the exact quantity of coffee consumed on each occasion with an exhaustive description of the cup from which it was taken. I left no personal details unconsidered from the patient's fingernails to the pimples on Mr. Weiss's nose.

But my tactics of studied tedium were a complete failure. The attempt to fatigue Thorndyke's brain with superabundant detail was like trying to surfeit a pelican with white bait. He consumed it all with calm enjoyment and asked for more; and when at last I did really begin to think that I had bored him a little, he staggered me by reading over his notes and starting a brisk cross-examination to elicit fresh facts! And the most surprising thing of all was that, when I had finished I seemed to know a great deal more about the case than I had ever known before.

"It was a very remarkable affair," he observed when the cross-examination was over, "a very suspicious affair with a highly unsatisfactory end. I am not sure that I entirely agree with your police officer. Nor do I fancy that some of my acquaintances at Scotland Yard would have agreed with him."

"Do you think I ought to have taken any further measures?" I asked uneasily.

"No; I don't see how you could. You did all that was possible under the circumstances. You gave the information, which is all that a private individual can do, especially if he is an overworked general practitioner. But still, an actual crime is the affair of every good citizen. I think we ought to take some action."

"You think there really was a crime then?"

"What else can one think? What do you think about it yourself?"

"I don't like to think about it at all. The recollection of that corpse-like figure in that gloomy bedroom has haunted me ever since I left the house. What do you suppose has happened?"

Thorndyke did not answer for a few seconds. At length he said gravely, "I am afraid, Jervis, that the answer to that question can be given in one word."

"Murder?" I asked with a slight shudder.

He nodded, and we were both silent for a while.

"The probability," he resumed after a pause, "that Mr. Graves is alive at this moment seems to me infinitesimal. There was evidently a conspiracy to murder him, and the deliberate, persistent manner in which that object was being pursued points to a very strong and definite motive. Then the tactics adopted point to considerable forethought and judgment. They are not the tactics of a fool or an ignoramus. We may criticize the closed carriage as a tactical mistake, calculated to arouse suspicion, but we have to weigh it against its alternative."

"What is that?"

"Well, consider the circumstances. Suppose Weiss had called you in the ordinary way. You would still have detected the use of poison. But now you could have located your man and made inquiries about him. You would probably have given the police a hint, and they would almost certainly have taken action, since they would have had the means of identifying the parties. The result would have been fatal to Weiss. The closed carriage invited suspicion, but it was a great safeguard. Weiss's methods were not so unsound after all. He is a cautious man, but cunning and very persistent."

"Which all leads to the probability that he has pursued his scheme and brought it to a successful end."

"I am afraid it does. But have you got your notes of the compass bearings?"

"The book is in my overcoat pocket with the board. I will fetch them."

I went into the office where our coats hung and brought back the notebook with the little board to which it was still attached by the rubber band. Thorndyke took them from me, and opening the book, ran his eye quickly down one page after another. Suddenly he glanced at the clock. "It is a little late to begin," he said, "but these notes look rather alluring. I am inclined to plot them out at once. I fancy from their appearance that they will enable us to locate the house without much difficulty. But don't you let me keep you up if you are tired. I can work them out by myself."

"You won't do anything of the kind," I exclaimed. "I am as keen on plotting them as you are, and besides, I want to see how it is done. It seems to be a rather useful accomplishment."

"It is," said Thorndyke. "In our work, the ability to make a rough but reliable sketch survey is often of great value. Have you looked over these notes?"

"No. I put the book away when I came in and have not looked at it since."

"It is a quaint document. You seem to be rich in railway bridges in those parts, and the route was certainly none of the most direct, as you noticed at the time. However, we will plot it out and then we shall see exactly what it looks like and whither it leads us."

He retired to the laboratory and presently returned with a T-square, a military protractor, a pair of dividers, and a large drawing board on which was pinned a sheet of paper.

"Now," said he, seating himself at the table with the board before him, "as to the method. You started from a known position and you arrived at a place the position of which is at present unknown. We shall fix the position of that spot by applying two factors, the distance that you traveled and the direction in which you were moving. The direction is given by the compass; and as the horse seems to have kept up a remarkably even pace, we can take time as representing distance. You seem to have been traveling at about eight miles an hour, that is, roughly a seventh of a mile in one minute. So if we take one inch as representing one minute, we shall be working with a scale of about seven inches to the mile."

"That doesn't sound very exact as to distance," I objected.

"It isn't. But that doesn't matter much. We have certain landmarks, such as these railway arches that you have noted, by which the actual distance can be settled after the route is plotted. You had better read out the entries, and opposite each, write a number for reference, so that we need not confuse the chart by writing details on it. I shall start near the middle of the board, as neither you nor I seem to have the slightest notion what your general direction was."

I laid the open notebook before me and read out the first entry:

"Eight fifty-eight. West by South. Start from home. Horse thirteen hands."

"You turned around at once, I understand," said Thorndyke, "so we draw no line in that direction. The next is? . . ."

"Eight fifty-eight minutes, thirty seconds. East by North. And the next is Eight fifty-nine. North-east."

"Then you traveled east by north about a fifteenth of a mile, and we shall put down half-an-inch on the chart. Then you turned northeast. How long did you go on?"

"Exactly a minute. The next entry is Nine. West-north-west."

"Then you traveled about the seventh of a mile in a north-easterly direction, and we draw a line an inch long at an angle of forty-five degrees to the right of the north and south line. From the end of that we carry a line at an angle of fifty-six and a quarter degrees to the left of the north and south line, and so on. The method is perfectly simple, you see."

"Perfectly. I quite understand it now."

I went back to my chair and continued to read out the entries from the notebook while Thorndyke laid off the lines of direction with the protractor, taking out the distances with the dividers from a scale of equal parts on the back of the instrument. As the work proceeded, I noticed from time to time, a smile of quiet amusement spread over my colleague's keen, attentive face, and at each new reference to a railway bridge he chuckled softly.

"What, again!" he laughed, as I recorded the passage of the fifth or sixth bridge. "It's like a game of croquet. Go on. What is the next?"

I went on reading out the notes until I came to the final one.

"'Nine twenty-four. Southeast. In covered way. Stop. Wooden gates closed.'"

Thorndyke ruled off the last line, remarking, "Then your covered way is on the south side of a street which bears northeast. So we complete our chart. Just look at your route, Jervis."

He held up the board with a quizzical smile and I stared in astonishment at the chart. The single line, which represented the route of the carriage, zigzagged in the most amazing manner, turning, returning and crossing itself repeatedly, evidently passing more than once down the same thoroughfares and terminating at a comparatively short distance from its commencement.

"Why!" I exclaimed, "the rascal must have lived quite near to Stillbury's house!"

Thorndyke measured with the dividers the distance between the starting and arriving points of the route and took it off from the scale.

"Five-eighths of a mile, roughly," he said. "You could have walked it in less than ten minutes. And now let us get out the map and see if we can give to each of those marvelously erratic lines a local habitation and a name."

He spread the map out on the table and placed our chart by its side.

"I think," said he, "you started from Lower Kennington Lane?"

"Yes, from this point," I replied, indicating the spot with a pencil.

"Then," said Thorndyke, "if we swing the chart round twenty degrees to correct the deviation of the compass, we can compare it with the map."

He set off with the protractor an angle of twenty degrees from the north and south line and turned the chart round to that extent. After closely scrutinizing the map and the chart and comparing the one with the other, he said, "By mere inspection it seems fairly easy to identify the thoroughfares that correspond to the lines of the chart. Take the part that is near your destination. At nine twenty-one you passed under a bridge, going westward. That would seem to be Glasshouse Street. Then you turned south, apparently along the Albert Embankment where you heard the tug's whistle. Then you heard a passenger train start on your left; that would be Vauxhall Station. Next you turned around due east and passed under a large railway bridge, which suggests the bridge that carries the station over Upper Kennington Lane. If that is so, your house should be on the south side of Upper Kennington Lane, some three hundred yards from the bridge. But we may as well test our inferences by one or two measurements."

"How can you do that if you don't know the exact scale of the chart?"

"I will show you," said Thorndyke. "We shall establish the true scale and that will form part of the proof."

He rapidly constructed on the upper blank part of the paper, a proportional diagram consisting of two intersecting lines with a single cross-line.

"This long line," he explained, "is the distance from Stillbury's house to the Vauxhall railway bridge as it appears on the chart; the shorter cross line is the same distance taken from the ordnance map. If our inference is correct and the chart is reasonably accurate, all the other distances will show a similar proportion. Let us try some of them. Take the distance from the Vauxhall Bridge to the Glasshouse Street Bridge."

He made the two measurements carefully, and as the point of the dividers came down almost precisely in the correct place on the diagram, he looked up at me.

"Considering the roughness of the method by which the chart was made, I think that is pretty conclusive, though, if you look at the various arches that you passed under and see how nearly they appear to follow the position of the Southwestern Railway line, you hardly need further proof. But I will take a few more proportional measurements for the satisfaction of proving the case by scientific methods before we proceed to verify our conclusions by a visit to the spot."

He took off one or two more distances, and on comparing them with the proportional distances on the map, found them in every case as nearly correct as could be expected.

"Yes," said Thorndyke, laying down the dividers, "I think we have narrowed down the locality of Mr. Weiss's house to a few yards in a known street. We shall get further help from your note of nine twenty-three thirty, which records a patch of newly laid asphalt extending up to the house."

"That new surface will be pretty well smoothed down by now," I objected.

"Not so very completely," answered Thorndyke. "It is only a little over a month ago, and there has been very little wet weather since. It may be smooth, but it will be easily distinguishable from the old."

"And do I understand that you propose to go and explore the neighborhood?"

"Undoubtedly I do. That is to say, I intend to convert the locality of this house into a definite address, which I think will now be perfectly easy unless we should have the bad luck to find more than one covered way. Even then, the difficulty would be trifling."

"And when you have ascertained where Mr. Weiss lives? What then?"

"That will depend on circumstances. I think we shall probably call at Scotland Yard and have a little talk with our old friend Mr. Superintendent Miller, unless for any reason it seems better to look into the case ourselves."

"When is this voyage of exploration to take place?"

Thorndyke considered this question, and taking out his pocketbook, glanced through his engagements.

"It seems to me," he said, "that tomorrow is a fairly free day. We could take the morning without neglecting other business. I suggest that we start immediately after breakfast. How will that suit my learned friend?"

"My time is yours," I replied, "and if you choose to waste it on matters that don't concern you, that's your affair."

"Then we will consider the arrangement to stand for tomorrow morning, or rather, for this morning, as I see that it is past twelve."

With this Thorndyke gathered up the chart and instruments, and we separated for the night.

CHAPTER 9

THE HOUSE OF MYSTERY

Half past nine on the following morning found us spinning along the Albert Embankment in a cab to the pleasant tinkle of the horse's bell. Thorndyke appeared to be in high spirits. He had put my notebook in his pocket before starting, and once or twice he took it out and looked over its pages. He made no reference to the object of our quest, and the few remarks that he uttered would have indicated that his thoughts were occupied with other matters.

Arriving at Vauxhall Station, we alighted and made our way to the bridge that spans Upper Kennington Lane near its junction with Harleyford Road.

"Here is our starting point," said Thorndyke. "From this place to the house is about three hundred yards—say four hundred and twenty paces—and at about two hundred paces we ought to reach your patch of new asphalt. Now, are you ready? If we keep step, we shall average our stride."

We started together at a good pace, stepping out with military regularity and counting aloud as we went. As we approached the hundred and ninety fourth pace, I observed Thorndyke nod towards the roadway a little ahead, and looking at it attentively as we approached, it was easy to see by the regularity of surface and lighter color, that it had recently been repaved.

Counting out the four hundred and twenty paces, we halted. Thorndyke turned to me with a smile of triumph.

"Not a bad estimate, Jervis," said he. "That will be your house if I am not much mistaken. There is no other building in sight."

He pointed to a narrow turning some dozen yards ahead, apparently the entrance to a stable and closed by a pair of massive wooden gates.

"Yes," I answered, "there can be no doubt that this is the place, but," I added, as we drew nearer, "the nest is empty! Do you see?"

I pointed to a sign that was stuck on the gate, bearing as I could see at this distance the inscription "For Rent."

"Here is a new, if not altogether unexpected, development," said Thorndyke, as we stood gazing at the sign, which set forth that "these premises, including stables and workshops," were "to be let on lease or otherwise," and referred inquirers to Messrs. Ryebody Brothers, House agents. "The question is, should we make a few inquiries of the agent, or should we get the keys and have a look at the inside of the house? I am inclined to do both, and the latter first, if Messrs. Ryebody Brothers will trust us with the keys."

We proceeded up the lane to the address given and entering the office, Thorndyke made his request somewhat to the surprise of the clerk. Thorndyke was not quite the kind of person whom one naturally associates with stables and workshops. However, there was no difficulty. As the clerk sorted out the keys from a bunch hanging from a hook, he remarked,

"I expect you will find the place in a rather dirty and neglected condition. The house has not been cleaned yet; it is just as it was left when the brokers took away the furniture."

"Was the last tenant evicted then?" Thorndyke asked.

"Oh, no. He had to leave rather unexpectedly to take up some business in Germany."

"I hope he paid his rent," said Thorndyke.

"Oh, yes. Trust us for that. But I should say that Mr. Weiss—that was his name—was a man of some means. He seemed to have plenty of money, though he always paid in notes. I don't fancy he had a banking account in this country. He hadn't been here more than about six or seven months, and he paid us a cash deposit in lieu of references when he first came."

"I think you said his name was Weiss. It wouldn't be H. Weiss by any chance?"

"I believe it was. But I can soon tell you."

He opened a drawer and consulted what looked like a book of receipt forms. "Yes, H. Weiss. Do you know him, sir?"

"I knew a Mr. H. Weiss some years ago. He came from Bremen, I remember."

"This Mr. Weiss has gone back to Hamburg," the clerk observed.

"Ah," said Thorndyke, "then it would seem not to be the same. My acquaintance was a fair man with a beard and a decidedly red nose, and he wore spectacles."

"That's the man. You've described him exactly," said the clerk, who was apparently rather easily satisfied in the matter of description.

"Dear me," said Thorndyke, "what a small world it is. Do you happen to have a note of his address in Hamburg?"

"I haven't," the clerk replied. "You see we're done with him, having got the rent though the house is not actually surrendered yet. Mr. Weiss's housekeeper still has the front door key. She doesn't start for Hamburg for a week or so, and meanwhile she keeps the key so that she can call every day and see if there are any letters."

"Indeed," said Thorndyke. "I wonder if he still has the same housekeeper."

"This lady is a German," replied the clerk, "with a regular jaw-twisting name. Sounded like Shallybang."

"Schallibaum. That is the lady. A fair woman with hardly any eyebrows and a pronounced cast in the left eye."

"Now that's very curious, sir," said the clerk. "It's the same name, and this is a fair woman with remarkably thin eyebrows. I remember, now that you mention it. But it can't be the same person. I have only seen her a few times and then only just for a minute or so, but I'm quite certain she had no cast in her eye. You can dye your hair or you can wear a wig or you can paint your face, but a squint is a squint. There's no faking a swivel eye."

Thorndyke laughed softly. "I suppose not. Are these the keys?"

"Yes, sir. The large one belongs to the wicket in the front gate. The other is the latchkey belonging to the side door. Mrs. Shallybang has the key of the front door."

"Thank you," said Thorndyke. He took the keys, to which a wooden label was attached, and we made our way back towards the house of mystery, discussing the clerk's statements as we went.

"A very communicative young gentleman," Thorndyke remarked. "He seemed quite pleased to relieve the monotony of office work with a little conversation. And I am sure I was very delighted to indulge him."

"He hadn't much to tell all the same," said I.

Thorndyke looked at me in surprise. "I don't know what you would have, Jervis, unless you expect casual strangers to present you with a ready-made body of evidence, fully classified, with all the inferences and implications stated. It seemed to me that he was a highly instructive young man."

"What did you learn from him?" I asked.

"Oh, come, Jervis," he protested. "Is that a fair question, under our present arrangement? However, I will mention a few points. We learn that about six or seven months ago, Mr. H. Weiss dropped from the clouds into Kennington Lane, and that he has now ascended from Kennington Lane back into the clouds. That is a useful piece of information. Then we learn that Mrs. Schallibaum has remained here, which might be of little importance if it were not for a very interesting corollary that it suggests."

"Which is?"

"I must leave you to consider the facts at your leisure, but you will have noticed the stated reason for her remaining behind. She is engaged in plugging up the one gaping hole in their armor. One of them has been indiscreet enough to give this address to some correspondent—probably a foreign correspondent. Now, as they obviously wish to leave no tracks, they cannot give their new address to the post office to have their letters forwarded. Yet on the other hand, a letter left in the box might establish such a connection as would enable them to be traced. Moreover, the letter might be of a kind that they would not wish to fall into the wrong hands. They would not have given this address except for some peculiar circumstances."

"True, especially if they took this house for the express purpose of committing a crime in it."

"Exactly. And then there is one other fact that you may have gathered from our young friend's remarks."

"What is that?"

"That a controllable squint is a very valuable asset to a person who wishes to avoid identification."

"Yes, I did note that. The fellow seemed to think that it was absolutely conclusive."

"And so would most people. We can all squint towards our noses, but no normal person can turn his eyes away from one another. My impression is that the presence or absence, as the case might be, of a divergent squint would be accepted as absolute disproof of identity. But here we are."

He inserted the key into the wicket of the large gate, and when we had stepped through into the covered way, he locked it from the inside.

"Why have you locked us in?" I asked, seeing that the wicket had a latch.

"Because," he replied, "if we now hear anyone on the premises, we shall know who it is. Only one person besides ourselves has a key."

His reply startled me somewhat. I stopped and looked at him. "That is a quaint situation, Thorndyke. I hadn't thought of it. Why, she may actually come to the house while we are here; in fact, she may be in the house at this moment."

"I hope not," said he. "We don't particularly want Mr. Weiss to be put on his guard, for I take it he is a pretty alert gentleman under any circumstances. If she does come, we had better keep out of sight. I think we will look over the house first. That is of the most interest to us. If the lady does happen to come while we are here, she may stay to show us over the place and keep an eye on us. So we will leave the stables to the last."

We walked down the entry to the side door where I had been admitted by Mrs. Schallibaum on the occasions of my previous visits. Thorndyke inserted the latchkey, and as soon as we were inside, shut the door and walked quickly through into the hall, where I followed him. He made straight for the front door, where he began very attentively to examine the letterbox. It was a massive wooden box, fitted with a lock of good quality and furnished with a wire grill through which one could inspect the interior.

"We are in luck, Jervis," Thorndyke remarked. "Our visit has been most happily timed. There is a letter in the box."

"Well," I said, "we can't get it out; and if we could, it would be hardly justifiable."

"I don't know," he replied, "that I am prepared to agree to either of those propositions, but I would rather not tamper with another person's letter, even if that person should happen to be a murderer. Perhaps we can get the information we want from the outside of the envelope."

He produced from his pocket a little electric lamp and pressing the button, threw a beam of light in through the grill. The letter was lying on the bottom of the box face upwards, so that the address could easily be read.

"Dr. H. Weiss," Thorndyke read aloud. "German stamp, postmark apparently Darmstadt. You notice that the 'Dr.' is printed and the rest written. What do you make of that?"

"I don't quite know. Do you think he is really a medical man?"

"Perhaps we had better finish our investigation in case we are disturbed and discuss the bearings of the facts afterwards. The name of the sender may be on the flap of the envelope. If it is not, I shall pick the lock and take out the letter. Have you got a probe about you?"

"Yes, by force of habit I am still carrying my pocket case."

I took the little case from my pocket and extracted from it a jointed probe of thick silver wire, screwed the two halves together and handed the completed instrument to Thorndyke who passed the slender rod through the grill and adroitly turned the letter over.

"Ha!" he exclaimed with deep satisfaction as the light fell on the reverse side of the envelope, "we are saved from the necessity of theft—Johann Schnitzler, Darmstadt. That is all that we need. The German police can do the rest if necessary."

He handed me back my probe, pocketed his lamp, and turned back into the dark, musty-smelling hall.

"Do you happen to know the name of Johann Schnitzler?" he asked.

I replied that I had no recollection of ever having heard the name before.

"Neither have I," said he, "but I think we may form a pretty shrewd guess as to his avocation. As you saw, the word 'Dr.' was printed on the envelope, leaving the rest of the address to be written by hand. The plain inference is that he is a person who habitually addresses letters to medical men, and as the style of the envelope and the lettering is commercial not personal, we may assume that he is engaged in some sort of trade. Now, what is a likely trade?"

"He might be an instrument maker or a drug manufacturer; more probably the latter, as there is an extensive drug and chemical industry in Germany, and as Mr. Weiss seemed to have more use for drugs than instruments."

"Yes, I think you are right, but we will look him up when we get home. And now we had better take a glance at the bedroom, that is, if you can remember which room it was."

"It was on the first floor," said I, "and the door by which I entered was just at the head of the stairs."

We ascended the two flights, and as we reached the landing, I halted.

"This was the door," I said and was about to turn the handle when Thorndyke caught me by the arm.

"One moment, Jervis," said he. "What do you make of this?"

He pointed to a spot near the bottom of the door where on close inspection, four good-sized screw holes were distinguishable. They had been neatly stopped with putty, and were so nearly the color of the grained and varnished woodwork as to be hardly visible.

"Evidently," I answered, "there has been a bolt there, though it seems a queer place to put one."

"Not at all," replied Thorndyke. "If you look up you will see that there was another at the top of the door, and as the lock is in the middle, they must have been highly effective. But there are one or two other points that strike me. First, you will notice that the bolts have been fixed on quite recently, for the paint that they covered is of the same grimy tint as that on the rest of the door. Next, they have been taken off, which seeing that they could hardly have been worth the trouble of removal, seems to suggest that the person who fixed them considered that their presence might appear remarkable, while the screw holes which have been so skillfully and carefully stopped, would be less conspicuous."

"Then, they were on the outside of the door—an unusual situation for bedroom bolts—and were of considerable size. They were long and thick."

"I can see, by the position of the screw holes that they were long, but how do you arrive at their thickness?"

"By the size of the holes in the jamb of the door. Those holes have been very carefully filled with wooden plugs, but you can make out their diameter, which is that of the bolts, and which is decidedly out of proportion for an ordinary bedroom door. Let me show you."

He flashed his lamp into the dark corner, and I was able to see distinctly the portentously large holes into which the bolts had fitted, and also to note the remarkable neatness with which they had been plugged.

"There was a second door, I remember," said I.

"Let us see if that was guarded in a similar manner."

We strode through the empty room, awakening dismal echoes as we trod the bare boards, and flung open the other door. At top and bottom, similar groups of screw holes showed that this also had been made secure, and that these bolts had been of the same very substantial character as the others.

Thorndyke turned away from the door with a slight frown.

"If we had any doubts," said he, "as to what has been going on in this house, these traces of massive fastenings would be almost enough to settle them."

"They might have been there before Weiss came," I suggested. "He only came about seven months ago, and there is no date on the screw holes."

"That is quite true. But when with their recent fixture you couple the facts that they have been removed, that very careful measures have been taken to obliterate the traces of their presence, and that they would have been indispensable for the commission of the crime that we are almost certain was being committed here, it looks like an excess of reason to seek other explanations."

"But," I objected, "what if the man, Graves, was really imprisoned? Could not he have smashed the window and called for help?"

"The window looks out on the yard, as you see, but I expect it was secured too."

He drew the massive, old-fashioned shutters out of their recess and closed them.

"Yes, here we are." He pointed to four groups of screw holes at the corners of the shutters, and once more producing his lamp, narrowly examined the insides of the recesses into which the shutters folded.

"The type of fastening is quite evident," said he. "An iron bar passed right across at the top and bottom and was secured by a padlock. You can see the mark the bar made in the recess when the shutters were folded. When these bars were fixed and padlocked and the bolts were shot, this room was as secure for a prisoner without tools as a prison cell."

We looked at one another for awhile without speaking, and I fancy that if Mr. H. Weiss could have seen our faces, he might have thought it desirable to seek some retreat even more remote than Hamburg.

"It was a diabolical affair, Jervis," Thorndyke said at length, in an ominously quiet and even gentle tone. "A sordid, callous, cold-blooded crime of a type that is to me utterly unforgivable. Of course, it may have failed. Mr. Graves may even now be alive. I shall make it my very special business to ascertain whether he is or not. And if he is not, I shall take it as a sacred duty to lay my hand on the man who has caused his death."

I looked at Thorndyke with something akin to awe. In the quiet unemotional tone of his voice, in his unruffled manner and the stony calm of his face, there was something much more impressive, more fateful than there could have been in the fiercest threats or the most passionate denunciations. I felt that in those softly spoken words he had pronounced the doom of the fugitive villain.

He turned away from the window and glanced around the empty room. It seemed that our discovery of the fastenings was all the information that it had to offer.

"It is a thousand pities," I remarked, "that we were·unable to look around before they moved out the furniture. We might have found some clue to the scoundrel's identity."

"Yes," replied Thorndyke. "There isn't much information to be gathered here, I am afraid. I see they have swept up the small litter from the floor and poked it under the grate. We will turn that over, as there seems to be nothing else, and then we'll look at the other rooms."

He raked out the little heap of rubbish with his stick and spread it out on the hearth. It certainly looked unpromising, being just such litter as may be swept up in any untidy room during a move. But Thorndyke went through it systematically, examining each item attentively, even to the local tradesmen's bills and empty paper bags, before laying them aside. Another rake of his stick scattered the bulky masses of crumpled paper and brought into view an object which he picked up with some eagerness. It was a portion of a pair of spectacles, which had apparently been trodden on, for the side bar was twisted and bent and the glass was shattered into fragments.

"This ought to give us a hint," said he. "It will probably have belonged either to Weiss or Graves, as Mrs. Schallibaum apparently did not wear glasses. Let us see if we can find the remainder."

We both groped carefully with our sticks amongst the rubbish, spreading it out on the hearth and removing the numerous pieces of crumpled paper. Our search was rewarded by the discovery of the second eyepiece of the spectacles, of which the glass was badly cracked but less shattered than the other. I also picked up two tiny sticks at which Thorndyke looked with deep interest before laying them on the mantelpiece.

"We will consider them presently," said he. "Let us finish with the spectacles first. You see that the left eyeglass is a concave cylindrical lens of some sort. We can make out that much from the fragments that remain, and we can measure the curvature when we get them home, although that will be easier if we can collect some more fragments and stick them together. The right eye is plain glass; that is quite evident. Then these will have belonged to your patient, Jervis. You said that the tremulous iris was in the right eye, I think."

"Yes," I replied. "These will be his spectacles, without doubt."

We succeeded eventually in recovering some seven or eight small fragments of the broken eyeglasses, which Thorndyke laid on the mantelpiece beside the little sticks.

I took up the latter to examine them again. "What are these things? Can you make anything of them?"

He looked at them thoughtfully for a few moments and then replied, "I don't think I will tell you what they are. You should find that out for yourself, and it will be well worth your while to do so. They are rather suggestive objects under the circumstances. But note their peculiarities. Both are portions of some smooth, stout reed. There is a long, thin stick—about six inches long—and a thicker piece only three inches in length. The longer piece has a little scrap of red paper stuck on at the end; apparently a portion of a label of some kind with an ornamental border. The other end of the stick has been broken off. The shorter, stouter stick has had its central cavity artificially enlarged so that it fits over the other to form a cap or sheath. Make a careful note of those facts and try to think what they probably mean. What would be the most likely use for an object of this kind? When you have ascertained that, you will have learned something new about this case. And now, to resume our investigation. Here is a very suggestive thing."

He picked up a small, wide-mouthed bottle and, held it up for my inspection. "Observe the fly sticking to the inside, and the name on the label, 'Fox, Russell Street, Covent Garden.' "

"I don't know Mr. Fox."

"Then I will inform you that he is a dealer in the materials for 'makeup,' theatrical or otherwise, and I will leave you to consider the bearing of this bottle on our present investigation. There doesn't seem to be anything else of interest here except for that screw, which you notice is about the size of those with which the bolts were fastened on the doors. I don't think it is worthwhile to uncover any of the holes to try it; we should learn nothing fresh."

He rose and, having kicked the discarded rubbish back under the grate, gathered up his gleanings from the mantelpiece, carefully bestowing the spectacles and the fragments of glass in the tin box that he appeared always to carry in his pocket, and wrapping the larger objects in his handkerchief.

"A poor collection," was his comment, as he returned the box and handkerchief to his pocket, "and yet not so poor as I had feared. Perhaps if we question them closely enough, these unlikely trifles may be made to tell us something worth learning after all. Shall we go into the other room?"

We passed out onto the landing and into the front room, where guided by experience we made straight for the fireplace. But the little heap of rubbish there contained nothing that even Thorndyke's inquisitive eye could view with interest. We wandered around the room, peering into the empty cupboards and scanning the floor and the corners, without discovering a single object or relic of the late occupants. In the course of my walk I halted by the window and was looking down into the street when Thorndyke called to me sharply, "Come away from the window, Jervis! Have you forgotten that Mrs. Schallibaum may be in the neighborhood at this moment?"

As a matter of fact I had entirely forgotten the matter, nor did it now strike me as anything but the remotest of possibilities. I replied to that effect.

"I don't agree with you," Thorndyke rejoined. "We have heard that she comes here to look for letters. Probably she comes every day. There is a good deal at stake remember. They cannot feel quite as secure as they would wish. Weiss must have seen the view you took of the case and must have had some uneasy moments thinking of what you might do. In fact, we may assume that the fear of you drove them out of the neighborhood, and that they are mighty anxious to get that letter and cut the last link that binds them to this house."

"I suppose that is so," I agreed, "and if the lady should happen to pass this way and should see me at the window and recognize me, she would certainly smell a rat."

"A rat?" exclaimed Thorndyke. "She would smell a whole pack of foxes, and Mr. H. Weiss would be more on his guard than ever."

We went down the stairs and went out by the side door and through the covered way into the yard at the back. The workshops were fastened with rusty padlocks that looked as if they had not been disturbed for months. The stables were empty; the coach house was vacant and presented no traces of recent use. We returned up the covered way, and I was about to close the side door, which Thorndyke had left ajar, when he stopped me.

"We'll have another look at the hall before we go," said he, and walking softly before me, he made his way to the front door. Producing his lamp, he threw a beam of light into the letterbox.

"Any more letters?" I asked.

"Any more?" he repeated. "Look for yourself."

I stooped and peered through the grill into the lighted interior.

The box was empty.

Thorndyke regarded me with a grim smile. "We have been caught, Jervis, I suspect," said he.

"I didn't hear the sound of the door, did you?"

"No, I didn't hear any sound at all, which makes me suspect that she did. We must leave very carefully. Which way do you want to go?"

"It seems to me," I replied, "that my best plan would be to take a bus to get out of the neighborhood as quickly as possible. If I go through Ravensden Street into Kennington Park Road, I can pick up a bus that will take me to the Mansion House where I can change for Kensington. I will ride on the top deck so that I can keep a look out for any other bus or cab that may be following."

"Yes," said Thorndyke, "that seems a good plan. I will walk with you and see that you get a fair start."

We walked briskly along the lane and through Ravensden Street to the Kennington Park Road. A bus was approaching from the south at a steady pace, and we halted at the corner to wait for it. Several people passed us in different directions, but none seemed to take any particular notice of us even though we observed them rather narrowly, especially the women. Then the bus crawled up. I sprang on board and ascended to the roof where I seated myself and surveyed the prospect to the rear. No one else got on and no cab or vehicle was in sight. I continued to watch Thorndyke as he stood sentinel at the corner, and noted that no one appeared to be making any effort to overtake the bus.

Presently my colleague waved his hand to me and turned back towards Vauxhall, and I decided that our precautions had been unnecessary and settled myself in a rather more comfortable position.

CHAPTER 10

THE HUNTER HUNTED

The ordinary pace of the bus was a rather sluggish trot, and in a thickly populated thoroughfare its speed was further reduced by frequent stops. Bearing these facts in mind, I gave an occasional backward glance as we jogged northward, though my attention soon began to wander from the possibility of pursuit to the incidents of our recent exploration.

It had not been difficult to see that Thorndyke was well pleased with the results of our search, but except for the letter—which undoubtedly opened up a channel for further inquiry and possible identification—I could not see that any of the traces of what we had found justified his satisfaction. There were the spectacles, for instance. They were almost certainly the pair worn by Mr. Graves. But what then?

As to the other objects, I could make nothing of them. The little sticks of reed evidently had some use that was known to Thorndyke and furnished by inference some kind of information about Weiss, Graves, or Mrs. Schallibaum. But I had never seen anything like them before, and they conveyed nothing whatever to me. Then the bottle that had seemed so significant to Thorndyke was to me quite uninforming. It did indeed suggest that some member of the household might be connected with the stage, but it gave no hint beyond that. Certainly that person was not Mr. Weiss, whose appearance was as remote from that of an actor as could well be imagined. At any rate, the bottle and its label gave me no more useful hint than that it might be worth while to call on Mr. Fox and make inquiries; and something told me very emphatically that this was not what it had conveyed to Thorndyke.

These reflections occupied me until the bus rumbled over London Bridge and up King William Street and joined the converging streams of traffic at the Mansion House. Here I got off and changed to a bus bound for Kensington on which I traveled westward pleasantly enough, looking down into the teeming streets and whiling away the time by meditating upon the very agreeable afternoon that I promised myself.

Instinct—of the kind that manifests itself especially about one o'clock in the afternoon—propelled me in the direction of Brompton Road, and landed me at a table in a large restaurant apparently adjusted to the needs of ladies who had come to engage in the feminine sport of shopping. Here, while waiting for my lunch, I sat idly scanning the morning paper and wondering what I should do with the rest of the day. Presently my eye caught the announcement of a matinee at the theater in Sloane Square. It was quite a long time since I had been to a theater, and as the play—a light comedy—seemed likely to satisfy my not very critical taste, I decided to devote the afternoon to reviving my acquaintance with the drama. And so as soon as my lunch was finished, I walked down the Brompton Road, stepped onto a bus, and was duly deposited at the door of the theater. A couple of minutes later I found myself occupying an excellent seat in the second row, oblivious to Thorndyke's words of warning.

I am not an enthusiastic playgoer. I do not go to a theater to be instructed. But, by way of compensation, I am not difficult to please. To a simple play, adjusted to my primitive taste, I can bring a certain simple appreciation that enables me to extract from the performance the maximum of enjoyment. When the final curtain fell and the audience rose, I turned to go with the feeling that I had spent a highly agreeable afternoon.

Emerging from the theater, borne on the outgoing stream, I presently found myself opposite the door of a tea-shop. Instinct—the five o'clock instinct this time—guided me in, for I am a creature of habit, especially of the tea habit. The unoccupied table to which I drifted was in a shady corner not very far from the cashier's desk, and here I had been seated less than a minute when a lady passed me on her way to her table. The glimpse that I caught of her as she approached—it was but a glimpse, since she passed behind me—showed that she was dressed in black, and that she wore a beaded veil and hat. In addition to the glass of milk and the bun that she carried, she was encumbered by an umbrella and a small basket apparently containing some kind of needlework. I must confess that I gave her very little attention at the time, being occupied in anxious speculation as to how long it would be before the fact of my presence would impinge on the consciousness of the waitress.

The exact time by the clock on the wall was three minutes and a quarter, at the expiration of which an anemic young woman sauntered up to the table and bestowed on me a glance of sullen interrogation, as if mutely demanding what I wanted. I humbly requested that I might be provided with a pot of tea, whereupon she turned on her heel—which was a good deal worn down—and reported my request to a lady behind a marble-topped counter.

It seemed that the counter lady took a lenient view of the case, for in less than four minutes the waitress returned and gloomily deposited on the table before me a teapot, a milk jug, a cup and saucer, and a jug of hot water. Then she once more departed in ill humor.

I had just given the tea in the pot a preliminary stir and was about to pour out the first cup when I felt someone bump lightly against my chair and heard something rattle on the floor. I turned quickly and perceived the lady, whom I had seen enter, stooping just behind my chair. It seemed that having finished her frugal meal she was on her way out when she had dropped her little basket, which had promptly disgorged its entire contents on the floor.

This particular basket had contained materials for Oriental bead work, and no sooner had it reached the floor than each item of its contents appeared to become possessed and impelled to travel at headlong speed to some remote and unapproachable corner as distant as possible from its fellows.

As the only man—and almost the only person—near, the duty of salvage agent manifestly fell upon me. Down I went on my hands and knees to grope under tables and chairs in reach of the scattered treasure. I recovered a ball of the thick thread from a dark and dirty corner and a multitude of the large beads from all parts of the compass. At length I came forth with a double handful of the treasure trove and a very lively appreciation of the resistant qualities of a cast-iron table when applied to the human cranium.

The owner of the lost and found property was greatly distressed by the accident and the trouble it had caused me; in fact she was quite needlessly agitated about it. The hand which held the basket into which I poured the rescued trash trembled visibly, and the brief glance that I bestowed on her as she murmured her thanks and apologies—with a very slight foreign accent—showed me that she was excessively pale. That much I could see plainly in spite of the rather dim light in this part of the shop and the beaded veil that covered her face. I could also see that she was a rather remarkable looking woman, with a great mass of harsh, black hair and very broad black eyebrows that nearly met above her nose and contrasted strikingly with the dead white of her skin. But, of course, I did not look at her intently. Having returned her property and received her acknowledgments, I resumed my seat and left her to go on her way.

I had once more grasped the handle of the teapot when I made a rather curious discovery. At the bottom of the teacup lay a single lump of sugar. To the majority of persons it would have meant nothing. They would have assumed that they had dropped it in and forgotten it and would have proceeded to pour out the tea. But it happened that I did not take sugar in my tea, so it followed that the lump had not been put in by me. Assuming that it had been carelessly dropped in by the waitress, I turned it out on the table, filled the cup, and took a tentative sip to test the temperature.

The cup was yet at my lips when I chanced to look into the mirror that faced my table. Of course it reflected the part of the shop that was behind me, including the cashier's desk at which the owner of the basket now stood paying for her refreshment. Between her and me was a chandelier which cast its light on my back but shone full on her face and her veil. I could see that she was looking at me steadily. She was, in fact, watching me intently and with a very curious expression—an expression of expectancy mingled with alarm. But this was not all. As I returned her intent look—which I could do unobserved since my reflected face was in deep shadow—I suddenly perceived that that steady gaze engaged her right eye only; the other eye was looking sharply towards her left shoulder. In short, she had a divergent squint of the left eye.

I put down my cup with a thrill of amazement and a sudden surge of suspicion and alarm. An instant's reflection reminded me that when she had spoken to me a few moments before, both her eyes had looked into mine without the slightest trace of a squint. My thoughts flew back to the lump of sugar, to the sip of tea that I had already swallowed, and hardly knowing what I intended, I started to my feet and turned to confront her. But as I rose, she snatched up her change and darted from the shop. Through the glass door, I saw her spring on to the footboard of a passing cab and give the driver some direction. I saw the man whip up his horse, and by the time I reached the door the cab was moving off swiftly towards Sloane Street.

I stood irresolute. I had not paid and could not run out of the shop without making a fuss, and my hat and stick were still on the rail opposite my seat. The woman ought to be followed, but I had no taste for the task. If the tea that I had swallowed was innocuous, no harm was done, and I was rid of my pursuer. So far as I was concerned, the incident was closed. I went back to my seat, and picking up the lump of sugar which still lay on the table where I had dropped it, put it carefully in my pocket. But my appetite for tea was satisfied for the present. Moreover it was hardly advisable to stay in the shop lest some fresh spy should come to see how I fared. Accordingly I obtained my check, handed it in at the cashier's desk, and took my departure.

All this time I had been taking it for granted that the lady in black had followed me from Kensington to this shop; that in fact she was none other than Mrs. Schallibaum. Indeed, the circumstances had rendered the conclusion inevitable. In the very instant when I had perceived the displacement of the left eye, complete recognition had come upon me. That the woman was Mrs. Schallibaum I now felt no doubt whatever.

Nevertheless, the whole affair was profoundly mysterious. The coarse, black hair might be her own, dyed, or it might be a wig. The eyebrows were made-up; it was a simple enough proceeding and made still simpler by the beaded veil. But how did she come to be there at all? How did she happen to be made-up in this fashion at this particular time? And, above all, how came she to be provided with a lump of what I had little doubt was poisoned sugar?

I turned over the events of the day, and the more I considered them the less comprehensible they appeared. No one had followed the bus either on foot or in a vehicle, as far as I could tell. Yet all the time, Mrs. Schallibaum must have been following. But how?

If I reached no satisfactory conclusion, my cogitations had one useful effect, they occupied my mind to the exclusion of that unfortunate sip of tea. The quantity that I had swallowed was not large—the tea being hotter than I cared for—and I remembered that when I had thrown out the lump of sugar, I had turned the cup upside down on the table; so there could have been nothing solid left in it. The lump of sugar was now in my pocket, reserved for careful examination at my leisure, and I reflected with a faint grin that it would be a little disconcerting if it should turn out to contain nothing but sugar after all.

On leaving the teashop I walked up Sloane Street with the intention of doing what I ought to have done earlier in the day. I was going to make perfectly sure that no spy was dogging my footsteps. But for my ridiculous confidence I could have done so quite easily before going to Endsley Gardens; and now, made wiser by a startling experience, I proceeded with systematic care. It was still broad daylight—for the lamps in the teashop had been rendered necessary only by the faulty construction of the premises. In an open space I could see far enough for complete safety. Arriving at the top of Sloane Street, I crossed and entered Hyde Park. Passing along the eastern shore, I entered one of the long paths that lead towards the Marble Arch and strode along it at such a pace as would make it necessary for any pursuer to hurry in order to keep me in sight. Halfway across the great stretch of turf, I halted for a few moments and noted the few people who were coming in my direction. Then I turned sharply to the left and headed straight for the Victoria Gate, but again, halfway, I turned off among a clump of trees, and standing behind the trunk of one of them took a fresh survey of the people who were moving along the paths. All were at a considerable distance and none appeared to be coming my way.

I now moved cautiously from one tree to another and passed through the wooded region to the south, crossed the bridge at a rapid walk and hurried along the south shore. From here I walked at the same rapid pace, inserting myself into the crowd with the skill born of long acquaintance with the London streets and began to zigzag amongst the narrow streets and courts of Soho. I passed through the many back streets and alleys and came out by Newcastle Street into the Strand, which I crossed immediately, ultimately entering the Temple by Devereux Court.

Even then I did not relax my precautions. From one court to another I passed quickly, loitering in those dark entries and unexpected passages that are known to so few but the regular Templars, and coming out into the open only at the last where the wide passage of King's Bench Walk admits no evasion. Halfway up the stairs, I stood for some time in the shadow, watching the approaches from the staircase window; and when at length I felt satisfied that I had taken every precaution that was possible, I inserted my key and let myself into our chambers.

Thorndyke had already arrived, and as I entered, he rose to greet me with an expression of evident relief.

"I am glad to see you, Jervis," he said. "I have been rather anxious about you."

"Why?" I asked.

"For several reasons. One is that you are the sole danger that threatens these people as far as they know. Another is that we made a most ridiculous mistake. We overlooked a fact that ought to have struck us instantly. But how have you fared?"

"Better than I deserved. That good lady stuck to me like a burr—at least I believe she did."

"I have no doubt she did. We have been caught napping, Jervis."

"How?"

"We'll go into that presently. Let us hear about your adventures first."

I gave him a full account of my movements from the time when we parted to that of my arrival home, omitting no incident that I was able to remember and, as far as I could, reconstituting my exceedingly devious homeward route.

"Your retreat was masterly," he remarked with a broad smile. "I should think that it would have utterly defeated any pursuer, and the only pity is that it was probably wasted on the desert air. Your pursuer had by that time become a fugitive. But you were wise to take these precautions, of course, for Weiss might have followed you."

"But I thought he was in Hamburg?"

"Did you? You are a very trusting young gentleman for a budding medical jurist. Of course we don't know that he is not, but the fact that he has given Hamburg as his present whereabouts establishes a strong presumption that he is somewhere else. I only hope that he has not located you, and from what you tell me of your later methods, I fancy that you would have shaken him off even if he had started to follow you from the tea shop."

"I hope so. But how did that woman manage to stick to me in that way? What was the mistake we made?"

Thorndyke laughed grimly. "It was a perfectly foolish mistake, Jervis. You started up Kennington Park Road on a leisurely omnibus, and neither you nor I remembered what there is underneath Kennington Park Road."

"Underneath!" I exclaimed, completely puzzled for the moment. Then, suddenly realizing what he meant, "Of course!" I exclaimed. "Idiot that I am. You mean the electric railway?"

"Yes. That explains everything. Mrs. Schallibaum must have watched us from some shop and quietly followed us up the lane. There was nothing to distinguish her from the other women unless you had recognized her, which you would hardly have been able to do at a fair distance. At least I think not."

"No," I agreed, "I certainly should not. In outdoor clothes and with a veil, I should never have been able to identify her without very close inspection. Besides, there was the disguise."

"Not at that time. She would hardly come disguised to her own house, for it might have led to her being challenged and asked who she was. I think we may take it that there was no actual disguise, although she would probably wear a hat and a veil, which would have prevented either of us from picking her out from the other women in the street. I think that she simply walked past us—probably on the other side of the road—as we stood waiting for the bus. She probably guessed that we were waiting for it and walked up the road in the direction in which it was going.

"Presently the bus would pass her, and there you were in full view on top keeping a vigilant lookout in the wrong direction. Then she would quicken her pace a little and in a minute or two would be in one of the electric trains whirling along under the street on which you were traveling. She would get out at the Borough Station, or she might take a more risky chance and go on to the Monument. But in any case she would wait for your bus, hail it, and get inside. I suppose you took up some passengers on the way?"

"Oh dear, yes. We were stopping every two or three minutes to take up or set down passengers, and most of them were women."

"Very well, then we may take it that when you arrived at the Mansion House, Mrs. Schallibaum was one of your inside passengers. It was a rather quaint situation, I think."

"What a couple of noodles she must have thought us!"

"No doubt. And that is the one consoling feature in the case. She will have taken us for a pair of absolute greenhorns. But to continue. Of course she traveled in your bus to

Kensington, thence she will have followed you to the restaurant and may even have lunched there."

"It is quite possible," said I. "The rooms were filled principally with women."

"Then she followed you to Sloane Street, and since you persisted in riding the upper berth, she could easily take a place inside. As to the theater, she must have taken it as a veritable gift, an arrangement made by you for her special convenience."

"Why?"

"My dear fellow, consider. She had only to follow you in and see you safely into your seat and there you were, left until called for. She could then go home, make up for her part, draw out a plan of action until the appointed time, then call and collect you."

"That is assuming a good deal," I objected.

"It is assuming, for instance, that she lives within a moderate distance of Sloane Square. Otherwise it would have been impossible."

"Exactly. You don't suppose that she goes about habitually with lumps of poisoned sugar in her pocket. And if not, then she must have got that lump from somewhere. Then the beads suggest a carefully prepared plan, and as I said just now, she can hardly have been madeup when she met us in Kennington Lane. From all of which it seems likely that her present abode is not very far from Sloane Square."

"At any rate," said I, "it was taking a considerable risk. I might have left the theater before she came back."

"Yes," Thorndyke agreed. "But it is like a woman to take chances. A man would probably have stuck to you when once he had got you off your guard. But she was ready to take chances. She chanced the railway; she chanced your remaining in the theater. She calculated on the probability of your getting tea when you came out, and she hit it off again. And then she took one chance too many; she assumed that you probably took sugar in your tea, and she was wrong."

"We are taking it for granted that the sugar was prepared," I remarked.

"Yes. Our explanation is hypothetical and may be entirely wrong. But it all hangs together, and if we find any poisonous matter in the sugar, it will be reasonable to assume that we are right. We will go up to the laboratory and make a preliminary test or two."

I took the lump of sugar from my pocket and gave it to him, and he carried it to the gas burner, by the light of which he examined it with a lens.

"I don't see any foreign crystals on the surface," said he, "but we had better make a solution and go to work systematically. If it contains any poison, we may assume that it will be some alkaloid, though I will test for arsenic too. You ought not to have carried this loose in your pocket. For legal purposes that would seriously interfere with its value as evidence. It doesn't matter much to us, as this analysis is only for our own information, and we can satisfy ourselves as to the state of your pocket. But bear the rule in mind another time."

We now ascended to the laboratory, where Thorndyke proceeded at once to dissolve the lump of sugar in a measured quantity of distilled water by the aid of gentle heat.

"Before we add any acid," he said, "or introduce any fresh matter, we will adopt the simple preliminary measure of tasting the solution. The sugar is a disturbing factor, but some of the alkaloids and most mineral poisons except for arsenic have a very characteristic taste."

He dipped a glass rod in the warm solution and applied it gingerly to his tongue.

"Ha!" he exclaimed, as he carefully wiped his mouth with his handkerchief, "simple methods are often very valuable. There isn't much doubt as to what is in that sugar. Let me recommend my learned brother to try the flavor. But be careful. A little of this will go a long way."

He took a fresh rod from the rack, dipped it in the solution, and handed it to me. I cautiously applied it to the tip of my tongue and was immediately aware of a peculiar tingling sensation accompanied by a feeling of numbness.

"Well," said Thorndyke; "what is it?"

"Aconite," I replied without hesitation.

"Yes," he agreed, "aconite it is. And that, I think, gives us all the information we want for now. I shall have a quantitative examination made later. You note the intensity of the taste, and you see what the strength of the solution is. Evidently that lump of sugar contained a very large dose of the poison. If the sugar had been dissolved in your tea, the quantity would have contained enough poison to lay you out within a few minutes, which would account for Mrs. Schallibaum's anxiety to get clear of the premises. She saw you drink from the cup, but I imagine she had not seen you turn the sugar out."

"Probably not, to judge by her expression. She looked terrified. She is not as hardened as her rascally companion."

"Which is fortunate for you, Jervis. If she had not been in such a fluster, she would have waited until you had poured your tea, and you would have got a poisonous dose before you noticed anything amiss."

"They are a pretty pair, Thorndyke," I exclaimed. "A human life seems to be no more to them than the life of a fly or a beetle."

"That is so. They are a standing menace to society. As long as they are at large, human lives are in danger, and it is our business to see that they do not remain at large a moment longer than is unavoidable. Which brings us to another point. You had better keep indoors for the next few days."

"Oh, nonsense," I protested. "I can take care of myself."

"I won't dispute that," said Thorndyke, "but this matter is of vital importance, and we can't be too careful. Yours is the only evidence that could convict these people. They know that and will stop at nothing to get rid of you, for by this time they will almost certainly have ascertained that the teashop plan has failed. Now your life is of some value to you, and you are the indispensable instrument for ridding society of these dangerous vermin."

"And how long," I asked, "am I to be held on parole?"

"Not long, I think. We have a very promising start. If I have any success, I shall be able to collect all the evidence I want in about a week. But there is an element of chance in some of it, which prevents me from giving a date. And it is just possible that I may have started on a false track. But that I shall be able to tell you better in a day or two."

"And I suppose," I said gloomily, "I shall be out of the hunt altogether?"

"Not at all," he replied, "You have got the Blackmore will to attend to. I shall hand you over all the documents and get you to make an orderly digest of the evidence. You will then have all the facts and can work out the case for yourself. Also I shall ask you to help Polton in some little operations which are designed to throw light into dark places and which you will find both entertaining and instructive."

"Oh, don't think I am complaining," I exclaimed.

"Tomorrow morning I shall give you my notes on the Blackmore case and the copies of the will and the depositions, from which you can draw up a digest of the evidence with remarks as to the conclusions that it suggests. Then there are our gleanings from New Inn to be looked over and considered; and with regard to this case, we have the fragments of a pair of spectacles which had better be put together into a rather more intelligible form in case we have to produce them in evidence. That will keep you occupied for a day or two, together with some work appertaining to other cases. And now let us dismiss professional topics. You have not dined and neither have I, but I dare say Polton has made arrangements for some sort of meal. We will go down and see."

We descended to the lower floor, where Thorndyke's anticipations were justified by a neatly laid table to which Polton was giving the finishing touches.

CHAPTER 11
THE BLACKMORE CASE REVIEWED

One of the conditions of medical practice is the capability of transferring one's attention at a moment's notice from one set of circumstances to another equally important but entirely unrelated. At each visit on his rounds the practitioner finds himself concerned with a particular, self-contained group of phenomena which he must consider at the moment with the utmost concentration, but which he must instantly dismiss from his mind as moves on to the next case. It is a difficult habit to acquire, for an important or distressing case is apt to take possession of the mind and hinder the attention that succeeding cases demand.

My first morning's work on the Blackmore will showed me that the same faculty is demanded in legal practice, and it also showed me that I had yet to acquire it. As I looked over the depositions and the copy of the will, memories of the mysterious house in Kennington Lane continually intruded into my reflections, and the figure of Mrs. Schallibaum, white-faced and terrified haunted me continually.

In truth, my interest in the Blackmore case was little more than academic, whereas in the Kennington case I was one of the parties and was personally concerned. To me, John Blackmore was but a name, Jeffrey but a shadowy figure to which I could assign no definite personality, and Stephen himself a casual stranger. Mr. Graves, on the other hand, was a real person. I had seen him in the tragic circumstances that had probably heralded his death. I had brought away with me a feeling of profound pity and concern as to his fate. The villain Weiss too, and the terrible woman who aided and abetted him, lived in my memory as vivid and dreadful realities. Although I had uttered no hint to Thorndyke, I lamented inwardly that I had not been given some work connected with this case, rather than with the dry, purely legal and utterly bewildering case of Jeffrey Blackmore's will.

Nevertheless, I stuck to my task. I read through the depositions and the will without getting a single glimmer of fresh light on the case, and I made a careful digest of all the facts. I compared my digest with Thorndyke's notes and found that, brief as they were, they contained several matters that I had overlooked. I drew up a brief account of our visit to New Inn with a list of the objects that we had observed or collected. And then I addressed myself to the statement of my conclusions from the facts set forth.

It was only when I came to make the attempt that I realized how completely I was at sea. In spite of Thorndyke's recommendation to study Marchmont's statement and of his hint that I would find something highly significant, I was borne irresistibly to one conclusion and one only—and the wrong one at that—that Jeffrey Blackmore's will was perfectly regular, sound, and valid.

I tried to attack the validity of the will from various directions and failed every time. Its genuineness was obviously not in question. There seemed to me only two conceivable objections that could be raised: the competency of Jeffrey to execute a will and the possibility of undue influence having been brought to bear on him.

With reference to the first, there was the apparent fact that Jeffrey was addicted to opium, and this might interfere with his competency to make a will. But had the drug habit produced such mental changes in the deceased as would compromise his judgment? There was not evidence in favor of any such belief. Up to the very end he had managed his own affairs, and if his habits of life had undergone a change, they were still the habits of a perfectly sane and responsible man.

The question of undue influence was more difficult. If it applied to any person in particular, that person could be none other than John Blackmore. Now it was an undoubted fact that, of all Jeffrey's acquaintance, his brother John was the only one who knew that he was in residence at New Inn. It was therefore possible that influence might have been brought to bear on the deceased. But there was no evidence that it had. The fact that the deceased man's only brother should be the one person who knew where he was living was not a remarkable one, and it had been satisfactorily explained by the necessity of Jeffrey's naming him as a reference for renting the chambers. And against the theory of undue influence was the fact that Jeffrey had voluntarily brought his will to the lodge and executed it in the presence of entirely disinterested witnesses.

In the end I had to give up in despair and, abandoning the documents, turned my attention to the facts elicited by our visit to New Inn.

Whatever Thorndyke might have observed on his own account, I had brought away from the dead man's chambers only a single fact. The cuneiform inscription was upside down. That was the sum of the evidence that I had collected; and the question was, what did it prove? To Thorndyke it conveyed some deep significance. But what?

The inverted position was not a mere temporary accident. It was hung on the wall, and the plates screwed on the frame showed that its position was permanent—that it had never hung in any other. That it could have been hung by Jeffrey himself was inconceivable. But allowing that it had been fixed in its present position when the new tenant moved in, the fact remained that there it had hung, presumably for months, and that Jeffrey Blackmore, with his expert knowledge of the cuneiform character, had never noticed that it was upside down. Or if he had noticed it, he had never taken the trouble to have it altered.

It seemed to me that the only conclusion deducible from the photograph was that it furnished a measure of the badness of the deceased man's vision—verging on total blindness. But there was nothing startlingly new in this. He had, himself, declared that he was fast losing his sight.

What was the bearing of his partial blindness on the will? If a man has eyesight sufficient to enable him to write out and sign a will, mere defective vision will not lead him to muddle the provisions. Yet something of this kind seemed to be in Thorndyke's mind, for now I recalled the question that he had put to the porter: "When you read the will over in Mr. Blackmore's presence, did you read it aloud?" That question could have but one significance. It implied a doubt as to whether the testator was fully aware of the exact nature of the document that he was signing. Yet if he was able to write and sign it, surely he was able also to read it through, to say nothing of the fact that, unless he was demented, he must have remembered what he had written.

Once again I had to confess myself beaten and in full agreement with Mr. Marchmont that "there was no case," that "there was nothing in dispute." Nevertheless, I carefully filed the copy that I had made of Thorndyke's notes, together with the notes on our visit to New Inn, and the few and unsatisfactory conclusions at which I had arrived. This brought me to the end of my first morning's work in my new capacity.

"And how," Thorndyke asked as we sat at lunch, "has my learned friend progressed? Does he propose that we advise Mr. Marchmont to enter a caveat?"

"I've read all the documents and boiled all the evidence down to a stiff jelly, and I am in a worse fog than ever."

"There seems to be a slight mixture of metaphors in my learned friend's remarks. But never mind the fog, Jervis. There is a certain virtue in fog. It serves, like a picture frame, to surround the essential with a neutral zone that separates it from the irrelevant."

"That is a very profound observation, Thorndyke," I remarked ironically.

"I was just thinking so myself," he rejoined.

"And if you could contrive to explain what it means—"

"That is unreasonable. By the way, I am going to introduce you to the gentle art of photography this afternoon. I am getting the loan of all the checks that were drawn by Jeffrey Blackmore during his residence at New Inn. There are only twenty-three of them all told, and I am going to photograph them."

"I shouldn't have thought the bank people would have let them go out of their possession."

"They are not going to. One of the partners, a Mr. Britton, is bringing them here himself and will be present while the photographs are being taken, so they will not go out of his custody. But, all the same, it is a great concession, and I should not have obtained it but for the fact that I have done a good deal of work for the bank and that Mr. Britton is a personal friend."

"How comes it that the checks are at the bank? Why were they not returned to Jeffrey in the usual way?"

"I understand from Britton," replied Thorndyke, "that all Jeffrey's checks were retained by the bank at his request. When he was traveling he used to leave his investment securities and other valuable documents in his bankers' custody. As he has never applied to have them returned, the bankers still have them and are retaining them until the will is proved. Then they will hand over everything to the executors."

"What is the object of photographing these checks?" I asked.

"There are several objects. First, since a good photograph is practically as good as the original, when we have the photographs we practically have the checks for reference. Then, since a photograph can be duplicated indefinitely, it is possible to perform experiments on it which involve its destruction; which would, of course, be impossible in the case of original checks."

"But the ultimate object, I mean. What are you going to prove?"

"You are incorrigible, Jervis," he exclaimed. "How should I know what I am going to prove? This is an investigation. If I knew the result beforehand, I wouldn't need to perform the experiment."

He looked at his watch, and, as we rose from the table, he said, "We had better go up to the laboratory and see that the apparatus is ready. Mr. Britton is a busy man, and we mustn't keep him waiting when he comes."

We ascended to the laboratory, where Polton was already busy inspecting the massively built camera. As I was to be inducted into the photographic art, I looked at it with more attention than I had ever done before.

"We're all ready, sir," said Polton, "Hallo! That's the downstairs bell. Shall I go, sir?"

"Perhaps you'd better," said Thorndyke. "It may not be Mr. Britton, and I don't want to be delayed just now."

However, it was Mr. Britton; an alert looking middle-aged man, who came in escorted by Polton and shook our hands cordially, having been previously told of my presence.

He carried a small but solid handbag to which he clung tena-ciously up to the very moment when its contents were required for use.

"So that is the camera," said he, running an inquisitive eye over the instrument. "Very fine one too; I am a bit of a photographer myself."

"Are you going to magnify these checks?" Mr. Britton asked.

"Not at first," replied Thorndyke.

"For convenience and speed I am going to photograph them half-size, so that six checks will go on one whole plate. Afterwards we can enlarge from the negatives as much as we like. But we would probably enlarge only the signatures in any case."

The precious bag was now opened, and the twenty-three checks were brought out and laid on the bench in a consecu-tive series in the order of their dates. Each batch was arranged so that the signatures were towards the middle. Thorndyke proceeded to focus the camera, and Polton inserted the plate and made the first exposure, carrying the plate off to develop while the next batch of checks was being fixed in position.

In his photographic technique, as in everything else, Polton followed as closely as he could the methods of his prin-cipal and instructor, methods characterized by that unhurried precision that leads to perfect accomplishment. When the first negative was brought forth, dripping, from the darkroom, it was without spot or stain, scratch or pinhole, uniform in color and of exactly the required density. The six checks shown on it looked as clear and sharp as fine etchings.

"Well," said Mr. Britton, when he finally returned his treasures to the bag, "you have now got twenty-three of our checks for all intents and purposes. I hope you are not going to make any unlawful use of them."

My colleague and I escorted our visitor down the stairs.

"I don't understand what you want the checks for," he remarked. "There is no question turning on signatures in the case of Blackmore deceased, is there?"

"I should say not," Thorndyke replied rather evasively.

"I should say very decidedly not," said Mr. Britton, "if I understood Marchmont aright. And even if there were, let me tell you, these signatures that you have got wouldn't help you. I have looked them over very closely, and I have seen a few signatures in my time, you know. There is an appreciable amount of variation; a very appreciable amount. But under the variation one can trace the personal character, the subtle, indescribable quality that makes it recognizable to the expert eye as Jeffrey Blackmore's writing. You understand me. There is such a quality, which remains when the coarser characteristics vary; just as a man may grow old, or fat, or bald and become quite changed; and yet through it all, he preserves a certain something, which makes him recognizable as a member of a particular family. Well, I find that quality in all those signatures, and so will you, if you have had enough experience of handwriting. I thought it best to mention it in case you might be giving yourself unnecessary trouble."

"It is very good of you," said Thorndyke, "and I need not say that the information is of great value, coming from such a highly expert source. As a matter of fact, your words will be of great value to me."

He shook hands with Mr. Britton, and as the latter disappeared down the stairs he turned into the sitting room and remarked, "That is a very significant observation, Jervis. I advise you to consider it attentively in all its bearings."

"You mean the fact that these signatures are undoubtedly genuine?"

"I meant the very interesting general truth that is contained in Britton's statement. A man carries his personal trademark, not in his face only, but in his nervous system and muscles, giving rise to characteristic movements and gait;

in his larynx, producing an individual voice; and even in his mouth, as shown by individual peculiarities of speech and accent. And the individual nervous system, by means of these characteristic movements, transfers its peculiarities to inanimate objects that are the products of such movements; as we see in pictures, in carving, in musical execution, and in handwriting. A particular specimen is the product of a particular set of motor skills guided by an individual brain."

"These are very interesting considerations, Thorndyke," I remarked, "but I don't quite see their present application. Do you mean them to bear in any special way on the Blackmore case?"

"I think they do bear on it very directly. I thought so while Mr. Britton was making his very illuminating remarks."

"I don't see how. In fact I cannot see why you are going into the question of the signatures at all. The signature on the will is admittedly genuine, and that seems to me to dispose of the whole affair."

"My dear Jervis," said he, "you and Marchmont are allowing yourselves to be obsessed by a particular fact. A very striking and weighty fact, I will admit, but still, only an isolated fact. Jeffrey Blackmore executed his will in a regular manner, complying with all the necessary formalities and conditions. In the face of that single circumstance you and Marchmont make a great mistake. You should never allow yourself to be bullied and browbeaten by a single fact."

"But," I protested, "this fact seems to be final. It covers all possibilities unless you can suggest any other that would cancel it."

"I could suggest a dozen," he replied. "Let us take an instance. Supposing Jeffrey executed this will for a wager; that he immediately revoked it and made a fresh will; that he placed the latter in the custody of some person, and that that person has suppressed it."

"Surely you do not make this suggestion seriously!" I exclaimed.

"Certainly I do not," he replied with a smile. "I merely give it as an instance to show that your final and absolute fact is really only conditional on there being no other fact that cancels it."

"Do you think he might have made a third will?"

"It is possible. A man who makes two wills may make three or more, but I may say that I see no present reason for assuming the existence of another will. What I want to impress on you is the necessity of considering all the facts instead of bumping heavily against the most conspicuous one and forgetting all the rest. By the way, here is a little problem for you. What was the object of which these are the parts?"

He pushed across the table a little cardboard box. In it were a number of very small pieces of broken glass, some of which had been cemented together by their edges.

"These, I suppose," said I, looking with considerable curiosity at the little collection, "are the pieces of glass that we picked up in poor Blackmore's bedroom?"

"Yes. You see that Polton has been endeavoring to reconstitute the object, whatever it was; but he has not been very successful, for the fragments were too small and the collection too incomplete. However, here is a specimen, built up of six small pieces, which exhibits the general character of the object fairly well."

He picked out the little irregularly shaped object and handed it to me. I could not but admire the neatness with which Polton had joined the tiny fragments together.

I took the little "restoration" and, holding it up before my eyes, moved it to and fro as I looked through it at the window.

"It was not a lens," I pronounced eventually.

"No," Thorndyke agreed, "it was not a lens."

"And so cannot have been an eyeglass. I would say that these are portions of a watch glass."

"That is Polton's opinion," said Thorndyke, "and I think you are both wrong."

"What do you say to the glass of a locket?"

"That is rather more probable, but it is not my view."

"What do you think it is?" I asked. But Thorndyke was not to be drawn out.

"I am submitting the problem for solution by you, my learned friend," he replied with an exasperating smile, and then added, "I don't say that you and Polton are wrong; only that I don't agree with you. Perhaps you had better make a note of the properties of this object and consider it at your leisure when you are ruminating on the other data referring to the Blackmore case."

"My ruminations," I said, "always lead me back to the same point."

"You mustn't let them," he replied. "Shuffle your data about. Invent hypotheses. Never mind if they seem rather wild. Don't put them aside on that account. Take the first hypothesis that you can invent and test it thoroughly with your facts. You will probably have to reject it, but you will be certain to have learned something new. Then try again with a fresh one. You remember what I told you of my methods when I began this branch of practice and had plenty of time on my hands?"

"I am not sure that I do."

"Well, I used to occupy my leisure in constructing imaginary cases, mostly criminal. For instance, I would devise an ingenious fraud and would plan it in detail, taking every precaution that I could think of against failure or detection, considering, and elaborately providing for every imaginable contingency. For the time being, my entire attention was concentrated on it, making it as perfect and secure and un-detectable as I could with the knowledge and ingenuity at my command. I behaved exactly as if I were proposing actually to carry it out, and my life or liberty depended on its success excepting that I made full notes of every detail of the scheme. Then, when my plans were as complete as I could make them, and I could think of no way in which to improve them, I changed sides and considered the case from the standpoint of detection. I analyzed the case, I picked out its inherent and unavoidable weaknesses, and especially I noted the respects in which a fraudulent proceeding of a particular kind differed from the bona fide proceeding that it simulated. The exercise was invaluable to me. I acquired as much experience from those imaginary cases as I should from real ones, and in addition I learned a method which is the one that I practice to this day."

"Do you mean that you still invent imaginary cases as mental exercises?"

"No; I mean that when I have a problem of any intricacy, I invent a case which fits the facts and the assumed motives of one of the parties. Then I work at that case until I find whether it leads to explanation or to some fundamental disagreement. In the latter case I reject it and begin the process over again."

"Doesn't that method sometimes involve a good deal of wasted time and energy?" I asked.

"No; because each time that you fail to establish a given case, you exclude a particular explanation of the facts and narrow down the field of inquiry. By repeating the process, you are bound to arrive at an imaginary case which fits all the facts. Then your imaginary case is the real case, and the problem is solved. Let me recommend that you give the method a trial."

I promised to do so, though with no very lively expectations as to the result, and with this, the subject was allowed for the present to drop.

CHAPTER 12

THE PORTRAIT

The state of mind which Thorndyke had advised me to cultivate was one that did not come easily. However much I shuffled the facts of the Blackmore case, the circumstances surrounding the execution of Jeffrey Blackmore's will intruded on the subject with hopeless persistency. In the midst of my praiseworthy efforts to construct some intelligible scheme of the case, that scene would make its appearance and reduce my mind to instant chaos.

For the next few days, Thorndyke was very much occupied with one or two other cases, which kept him in court during each trial. When he came home, he seemed unable to talk on professional topics. Meanwhile, Polton worked steadily at the photographs of the signatures, and with a view to gaining experience, I assisted him and watched his methods.

The signatures were enlarged from their original dimensions of less than an inch and a half in length to a length of four and a half inches, which rendered all the small peculiarities of the handwriting surprisingly distinct. Each signature was eventually mounted on a card bearing a number and the date of the check so that it was possible to place any two signatures together for comparison. I looked over the whole series and carefully compared those that showed any differences, but without discovering anything more than might have been expected in view of Mr. Britton's statement. There were some trifling variations, but they were all very much alike, and no one could doubt that the same hand wrote them all.

As this was apparently not in dispute, it furnished no new information. Thorndyke's object must be to test something apart from the genuineness of the signatures. But what could that something be? I dared not ask him, for questions of that kind were anathema, so there was nothing to do but to lie low and see what he would do with the photographs.

The whole series was finished on the fourth morning after my adventure at Sloane Square, and the pack of cards was duly delivered by Polton when he brought in the breakfast tray. Thorndyke took up the pack, and as he ran through them, I noticed that the number had increased from twenty-three to twenty-four.

"The additional one," Thorndyke explained, "is the signature to the first will, which was in Marchmont's possession. I have added it to the collection as it carries us back to an earlier date. The signature of the second will presumably resembles those of the checks drawn about the same date. But that is not material, or if it should become so, we could examine the second will."

He laid the cards out on the table in the order of their dates and slowly ran his eye down the series. I watched him closely and ventured presently to ask, "Do you agree with Mr. Britton as to the general identity of character in the whole set of signatures?"

"Yes," he replied. "I should certainly have put them down as being all the signatures of one person. The variations are very slight. The later signatures are a little stiffer, a little more shaky and indistinct, and the B's and k's are both appreciably different from those in the earlier ones. But there is another fact which emerges when the whole series is seen together, and it is so striking and significant a fact that I am astonished at its not having been remarked on by Mr. Britton."

"Indeed!" said I, stooping to examine the photographs with fresh interest. "What is that?"

"It is a very simple fact and very obvious, and yet, as I have said, very significant. Look carefully at number one, which is the signature of the first will, dated three years ago, and compare it with number three, dated the eighteenth of September last year."

"They look to me identical," said I, after a careful comparison.

"So they do to me," said Thorndyke. "Neither of them shows the change that occurred later. But if you look at number two, dated the sixteenth of September, you will see that it is in the later style. So is number four dated the twenty-third of September; but numbers five and six, both at the beginning of October, are in the earlier style, like the signature of the will. Thereafter all the signatures are in the new style. But if you compare number two, dated the sixteenth of September, with number twenty-four, dated the fourteenth of March this of year—the day of Jeffrey's death—you see that they exhibit no difference. Both are in the later style, but the last shows no greater change than the first."

I reflected a few moments, trying to make out the deep significance to which Thorndyke was directing my attention and not succeeding very triumphantly.

"You mean," I said, "that the occasional reversions to the earlier form convey some material suggestion?"

"Yes; but more than that. What we learn from an inspection of this series is this: that there was a change in the character of the signature; a very slight change, but quite recognizable. That change was not gradual nor was it progressive.

It occurred at a certain definite time. At first there were one or two reversions to the earlier form, but after number six the new style continued to the end; and you notice that it continued without any increase in the change and without any variation. There are no intermediate forms. Some of the signatures are in the old style and some in the new, but there are none that are half and half. So what we have are two types of his signature, very much alike, but distinguishable. The change occurs abruptly, but shows no tendency to increase as time goes on. It is not a progressive change."

"It is remarkable," I said, poring over the cards to verify Thorndyke's statements. "I don't quite know what to make of it."

"Still," said Thorndyke, "there must be some explanation of the change in the character of the signatures, and that explanation cannot be the failing eyesight of the writer, for that is a gradually progressive and continuous condition, whereas the change in the writing is abrupt and intermittent."

I considered Thorndyke's remark for a few moments, and then a light—though not a very brilliant one—seemed to break on me.

"I think I see what you are driving at," said I. "You mean that the change in the writing must be associated with some new condition affecting the writer, and that that condition existed intermittently."

Thorndyke nodded approvingly, and I continued, "The only intermittent condition that we know of is the effect of opium. So we might consider the clearer signatures to have been made when Jeffrey was in his normal state, and the less distinct ones after a bout of opium smoking."

"That is perfectly sound reasoning," said Thorndyke. "What further conclusion does it lead to?"

"It suggests that the opium habit had been only recently acquired, since the change was noticed only about the time he went to live at New Inn. Since the change in the writing is at first intermittent and then continuous, we may infer that the opium smoking was at first occasional and later became a confirmed habit."

"Quite a reasonable conclusion and very clearly stated," said Thorndyke. "I don't say that I entirely agree with you, or that you have exhausted the information that these signatures offer. But you have started in the right direction."

"I may be on the right road," I said gloomily, "but I am stuck fast in one place, and I see no chance of getting any farther."

"But you have a quantity of data," said Thorndyke. "You have all the facts that I had to start with from which I constructed the hypothesis that I am now busily engaged in verifying. Shall we tabulate the facts that are in our joint possession and see what they suggest?"

I grasped eagerly at the offer, though I had combed over my notes again and again. Thorndyke produced a slip of paper from a drawer and, uncapping his fountain pen, proceeded to write down the leading facts, reading each aloud as soon as it was written.

"1. The second will was unnecessary since it contained no new matter, expressed no new intentions, and met no new conditions. The first will was quite clear and efficient.

"2. The evident intention of the testator was to leave the bulk of his property to Stephen Blackmore.

"3. The second will did not, under existing circumstances, give effect to this intention, whereas the first will did.

"4. The signature of the second will differs slightly from that of the first, and also from what had hitherto been the testator's ordinary signature.

"And now we come to a very curious group of dates which I will advise you to consider with great attention.

"5. Mrs. Wilson made her will at the beginning of September last year without acquainting Jeffrey Blackmore, who seems to have been unaware of the existence of this will.

"6. His own second will was dated the twelfth of November of last year.

"7. Mrs. Wilson died of cancer on the twelfth of March this present year.

"8. Jeffrey Blackmore was last seen alive on the fourteenth of March.

"9. His body was discovered on the fifteenth of March.

"10. The change in the character of his signature began about September last year and became permanent after the middle of October.

"You will find that collection of facts reward careful study, Jervis, especially when considered in relation to the further data.

"11. We found in Blackmore's chambers a framed inscription of large size, hung upside down, as well as what appeared to be the remains of a watch glass and a box of candles and some other objects."

He passed the paper to me and I pored over it intently, focusing my attention on the various items with all the power of my will. But struggle as I would, no general conclusion could be made to emerge from the mass of apparently disconnected facts.

"Well?" Thorndyke said presently, after watching with grave interest my unavailing efforts, "what do you make of it?"

"Nothing!" I exclaimed desperately, slapping the paper down on the table. "Of course, I can see that there are some queer coincidences. But how do they bear on the case? I understand that you want to upset this will which we know to have been signed without compulsion or even suggestion in the presence of two respectable men who have sworn to the identity of the document. That is your object, I believe?"

"Certainly it is."

"Then I am confounded to see how you are going to do it. Not, I should say, by offering a group of vague coincidences that would muddle any brain but your own."

Thorndyke chuckled softly but pursued the subject no further.

"Put that paper in your file with your other notes," he said, "and think it over at your leisure. And now I want a little help from you. Have you a good memory for faces?"

"Fairly good, I think. Why?"

"Because I have a photograph of a man whom I think you may have met. Just look at it and tell me if you remember the face."

He drew a large photograph from an envelope that had come by the morning's post and handed it to me.

"I have certainly seen this face somewhere," said I, taking the portrait over to the window to examine it more thoroughly, "but I can't at the moment remember where."

"Try," said Thorndyke. "If you have seen the face before, you should be able to recall the person."

I looked intently at the photograph, and the more I looked, the more familiar did the face appear. Suddenly the identity of the man flashed into my mind and I exclaimed in astonishment, "It can't be that poor creature at Kennington, Mr. Graves?"

"I think it can," replied Thorndyke, "and I think it is. But could you swear to the identity in a court of law?"

"It is my firm conviction that the photograph is that of Mr. Graves. I would swear only to that."

"No man ought to swear to more," said Thorndyke. "Identification is always a matter of opinion or belief. I think your sworn testimony would be sufficient."

It is needless to say that the production of this photograph filled me with amazement and curiosity as to how Thorndyke had obtained it. But, as he replaced it impassively in its envelope without volunteering any explanation, I felt that I could not question him directly. Nevertheless, I ventured to approach the subject in an indirect manner.

"Did you get any information from those Darmstadt people?" I asked.

"Schnitzler? Yes. I learned that Dr. H. Weiss was a stranger to them; that they knew nothing about him except that he had ordered from them and been supplied with a hundred grams of pure hydrochloride of morphine."

"All at once?"

"No. In separate parcels of twenty-five grams each."

"Is that all you know about Weiss?"

"It is all that I actually know, but it is not all that I suspect . . . on very substantial grounds. By the way, what did you think of the coachman?"

"I don't know that I thought very much about him. Why?"

"You never suspected that he and Weiss were one and the same person?"

"No. They weren't in the least alike. And one was a Scotchman and the other a German. But perhaps you know that they were the same?"

"I only know what you have told me. But considering that you never saw them together, that the coachman was never available for messages or assistance when Weiss was with you, that Weiss always made his appearance some time after you arrived and disappeared some time before you left, it has seemed to me that they might have been the same person."

"I would say it was impossible. They were so very different in appearance. But supposing that they were the same, would the fact be of any importance?"

"It would mean that we could save ourselves the trouble of looking for the coachman. And it would suggest some inferences, which will occur to you if you think the matter over.

But being only a speculative opinion at present, it would not be safe to infer very much from it."

"I had no idea that you were in possession of enough facts to enable you to get any further with it."

"But you knew all the very striking facts of the case, and you saw the additional evidence that we extracted from the empty house."

"Do you mean those things that we picked out from the rubbish under the grate?" I said.

"Yes. You saw those curious little pieces of reed and the pair of spectacles. They are lying in the top drawer of that cabinet at this moment, and I recommend you to have another look at them. To me they were most instructive."

"Unfortunately," said I, "the pieces of reed convey nothing to me. I don't know what they are or of what they have formed a part."

"I think," he replied, "that if you examine them with due consideration, you will find their use pretty obvious. Have a good look at them and the spectacles too. Think over all that you know of that mysterious group of people who lived in that house, and see if you cannot form some coherent theory of their actions. You will have a quiet day, as I shall not be home until the evening. Set yourself this task. I assure you that you have the material for identifying—or rather for testing the identity of—at least one of those persons. Let me know in the evening what further investigations you would propose."

"Very well," said I. "It shall be done according to your word. I will addle my brain afresh with the affair of Mr. Weiss and his patient, and let the Blackmore case wait."

"There is no need to do that. You have a whole day before you. An hour's really close consideration of the Kennington case ought to show you what your next move should be, and then you could devote yourself to the consideration of Jeffrey Blackmore's will."

With this final piece of advice, Thorndyke collected the papers for his day's work, and took his departure, leaving me to my meditations.

CHAPTER 13
THE STATEMENT OF SAMUEL WILKINS

As soon as I was alone, I opened the drawer and took from it the two pieces of reed and the shattered remains of the spectacles and laid them on the table. The repairs that Thorndyke had contemplated in the case of the spectacles had not been made. Apparently they had not been necessary. The battered wreck that lay before me had evidently furnished the necessary information, for since Thorndyke was in possession of a portrait of Mr. Graves, it was clear that he had succeeded in identifying him so far as to get into communication with someone who had known him intimately.

The circumstance should have been encouraging. But somehow it was not. What was possible to Thorndyke was "theoretically" possible to me or to any one else. But Thorndyke's brain was not an ordinary brain. Facts which his mind instantly perceived remained unconnected and without meaning to other people. He seemed to take in everything at a single glance and in an instant to appreciate the meaning of everything that he had seen.

Here was a case in point. I had myself seen all that he had seen, and indeed much more, for I had looked on the very people and witnessed their actions, whereas he had never set eyes on any of them. I had examined the little handful of rubbish that he had gathered up so carefully and would have flung it back under the grate without a qualm. And yet Thorndyke had managed to piece together facts so completely that he had already, in these few days, narrowed down the field of inquiry to quite a small area.

From these reflections I returned to the objects on the table. The spectacles were not so profound a mystery to me. A pair of spectacles might easily afford good evidence for identification, that I perceived clearly enough—especially a pair constructed by a skilled optician to remedy a particular defect of vision and to fit a particular face. And such were the spectacles before me.

I could easily make out from the fragments that one glass had been cut to a prescribed shape and almost certainly ground to a particular formula. Hence these spectacles had an individual character, but it was impossible to inquire of all the spectacle makers in Europe—for the glasses were not necessarily made in England. As confirmation the spectacles might be valuable; as a starting point they were of no use at all.

From the spectacles I turned to the pieces of reed. These were what had given Thorndyke his start. Would they give me a leading hint too? I looked at them and wondered what it was that they had told Thorndyke. The little fragment of the red paper label had a dark brown or thin black border ornamented with a pattern, and on it I detected a couple of tiny points of gold like the dust from leaf-gilding. But I learned nothing from that. The shorter piece of reed was artificially hollowed to fit on the longer piece. Apparently it formed a cap. But what did it protect? A point or edge of some kind? Could this be a pocketknife of any sort? No, the material was too fragile for a knife handle. It could not be an etching needle for the same reason, and it was not a surgical appliance. At least it was not like any surgical instrument that was known to me.

I turned it over and over, and then I had a brilliant idea. Was it a reed pen from which the point had been broken off? I knew that reed pens were still in use by some draftsmen. Could any of our friends be draftsmen? This seemed the most probable solution, and the more I thought about it the more likely it seemed. Could it be that Mr. Graves was an illustrator, and that Thorndyke had established his identity by looking through the works of the known draftsmen?

This problem occupied me for the rest of the day. My explanation did not seem quite to fit Thorndyke's description of his methods, but I could think of no other. I turned it over during my solitary lunch; I meditated on it in the afternoon, and having refreshed my brain with a cup of tea, I went forth to walk in the Temple gardens—which I was permitted to do without breaking my parole—to think it out afresh.

The result was disappointing. I was basing my reasoning on the assumption that the pieces of reed were parts of a particular appliance, pertaining to a particular craft, whereas they might be the remains of something quite different, appertaining to a totally different craft or to no craft at all. And in no case did they point to any known individual or indicate any but the vaguest kind of search. After pacing the pleasant walks for nearly two hours, I turned back towards our chambers.

My fruitless speculations had left me somewhat irritable. The lighted windows that I had noticed as I approached had given me the impression that Thorndyke had returned. I had intended to press him for a little further information. But when I let myself into our chambers and found instead of my colleague, a total stranger—and only a back view at that—I was disappointed and annoyed.

The stranger was seated by the table, reading a large document that looked like a lease. He made no movement when I entered, but when I crossed the room and wished him

"Good evening," he half rose and bowed silently. It was then that I first saw his face, and a mighty start he gave me. For one moment I actually thought he was Mr. Weiss, so close was the resemblance, but immediately I perceived that he was a much smaller man.

I sat down nearly opposite and stole an occasional furtive glance at him. The resemblance to Weiss was really remarkable. The same flaxen hair, the same ragged beard and a similar patchy red nose. He wore spectacles too, through which he took a quick glance at me now and again, returning immediately to his document.

After some moments of rather embarrassing silence, I ventured to remark that it was a mild evening, to which he assented with a sort of "hm-hm" and nodded slowly. Then came another interval of silence, during which I speculated on the possibility of his being a relative of Mr. Weiss and wondered what he was doing in our chambers.

"Have you an appointment with Dr. Thorndyke?" I asked at length.

He bowed solemnly and by way of reply emitted another "hm-hm."

I looked at him sharply, a little nettled by his lack of manners, whereupon he opened out the lease so that it screened his face, and as I glanced at the back of the document, I was astonished to observe that it was shaking rapidly.

The fellow was actually laughing! What he found in my simple question to cause him so much amusement I was totally unable to imagine. But there it was. The tremulous movements of the document left me in no possible doubt that he was for some reason convulsed with laughter.

It was extremely mysterious. It was rather embarrassing. I took out my pocket file and began to look over my notes. Then the document was lowered, and I was able to get another look at the stranger's face. He was really extraordinarily like Weiss. The shaggy eyebrows, throwing the eye sockets into shadow, gave him the same owlish, solemn expression that I had noticed in my Kennington acquaintance—which, by the way, was singularly out of character with the frivolous behavior that I had just witnessed.

From time to time as I looked at him, he caught my eye and instantly averted his own, turning rather red. Apparently he was a shy, nervous man, which might account for his giggling. And it seemed my own eye had this disconcerting quality, for even as I looked at him, the document suddenly went up again and began to shake violently.

I stood it for a minute or two, but finding the situation intolerably embarrassing, I rose and brusquely excused myself. I went up to the laboratory to look for Polton and inquire at what time Thorndyke was expected home. To my surprise, however, I discovered Thorndyke himself just finishing the mounting of a microscopic specimen.

"Did you know that there is someone below waiting to see you?" I asked.

"Is it any one you know?" he inquired.

"No," I answered. "It is a red-nosed, sniggering fool in spectacles. He has got a lease or a deed or some other sort of document, which he has been using to play a sort of idiotic game of peek-a-boo! I couldn't stand it, so I came up here."

Thorndyke laughed heartily at my description of his client.

"What are you laughing at?" I asked sourly. He laughed yet more heartily and added to the aggravation by wiping his eyes.

"Our friend seems to have put you out," he remarked.

"He put me out literally. If I had stayed much longer, I should have punched his head."

"In that case," said Thorndyke, "I am glad you didn't stay. But come down and let me introduce you."

"No, thank you. I've had enough of him for the present."

"But I have a very special reason for wishing to introduce you. I think you will get some information from him that will interest you very much, and you needn't quarrel with a man for being of a cheerful disposition."

"Cheerful!" I exclaimed. "I don't call a man cheerful because he behaves like a gibbering idiot."

To this Thorndyke made no reply but a broad and appreciative smile. We descended to the lower floor. As we entered the room, the stranger rose, and glancing in an embarrassed way from one of us to the other, suddenly broke out into an undeniable snigger. I looked at him sternly, and Thorndyke, quite unmoved by his indecorous behavior, said in a grave voice, "Let me introduce you, Jervis, though I think you have met this gentleman before."

"I think not," I said stiffly.

"Oh yes, you have, sir," interposed the stranger, and as he spoke, I started. The voice was uncommonly like the familiar voice of Polton.

I looked at the speaker with sudden suspicion. And now I could see that the flaxen hair was a wig, that the beard had a decidedly artificial look, and that the eyes that beamed through the spectacles were remarkably like the eyes of our assistant. But the blotchy face, the bulbous nose and the shaggy, overhanging eyebrows were alien features that I could not reconcile with the personality of our refined and aristocratic-looking little assistant.

"Is this a practical joke?" I asked.

"No," replied Thorndyke. "It is a demonstration. When we were talking this morning it appeared to me that you did not realize the extent to which it is possible to conceal identity under suitable conditions of light. So I arranged, with Polton's rather reluctant assistance, to give you visible evidence. The conditions are not favorable, which makes the demonstration more convincing. This is a very well-lighted room, and Polton is a very poor actor. In spite of this, it has been possible for you to sit opposite him for several minutes and look at him—no doubt attentively—without discovering his identity. If the room had been lighted only with a candle and Polton had been equal to the task of supporting his makeup with an appropriate voice and manner, the deception would have been perfect."

"I can see quite plainly that he has a wig on," said I.

"Yes; but you would not in a dimly lighted room. On the other hand, if Polton were to walk down Fleet Street at midday in this condition, the makeup would be conspicuously evident to any moderately observant passerby. The secret consists in a careful adjustment to the conditions of light and distance in which the makeup is to be seen. That in use on the stage would look ridiculous in an ordinary room; that which would serve in an artificially lighted room would look ridiculous out of doors by daylight."

"Is any effective makeup possible out of doors in ordinary daylight?" I asked.

"Oh, yes, but it must be on a totally different scale from that of the stage. A wig, and especially a beard or moustache, must be joined carefully at the edges. The eyebrows and color of the skin must be applied much more subtly. Polton's nose has been built up with a small covering of toupee paste, and the general tinting has been done with greasepaint with a very light scumble of powder color to take off some of the shine. You would be surprised to see how little paste is required to alter the shape of the nose and the entire character of the face."

At this moment there came a loud knock at the door, a single, solid rap of the knocker which Polton seemed to recognize, for he shouted, "Oh dear, sir! That'll be Wilkins, the cabman! I'd forgotten all about him. Whatever's to be done?"

He stared at us in ludicrous horror for a moment or two, and then snatching off his wig, beard and spectacles, poked them into a cupboard. But his appearance was now too much even for Thorndyke—who hastily got behind him—for he had now resumed his ordinary personality, but with a very material difference.

"Oh, it's nothing to laugh at, sir," he exclaimed indignantly as I crammed my handkerchief into my mouth. "Somebody's got to let him in, or he'll go away."

"Yes, and that won't do," said Thorndyke. "But don't worry, Polton. You can step into the office. I'll see to the door."

As the door opened, a thick and husky voice inquired, "Gent of the name of Polton live here?"

"Yes, quite right," said Thorndyke. "Come in. Your name is Wilkins, I think?"

"That's me, sir," said the voice; and in response to Thorndyke's invitation, a typical cabman stalked into the room, and glancing around with a mixture of embarrassment and defiance, suddenly fixed on Polton's nose a look of devouring curiosity.

"Here you are, then," Polton remarked nervously.

"Yus," replied the cabman in a slightly hostile tone. "Here I am. What am I wanted to do? And where's this here Mr. Polton?"

"I am Mr. Polton," replied our abashed assistant.

"Well, it's the other Mr. Polton what I want," said the cabman, with his eyes still riveted on the olfactory prominence.

"There isn't any other Mr. Polton," our man replied irritably. "I am the . . . er . . . person who spoke to you in the shelter."

"Are you though?" said the incredulous cabby. "I shouldn't have thought it, but you ought to know. What do you want me to do?"

"We want you," said Thorndyke, "to answer one or two questions."

Polton silently slipped out of the room.

"Your name, I think, is Wilkins?" said Thorndyke.

"That's me, sir. Samuel Wilkins is my name."

"And your occupation?"

"Is a very tryin' one and not paid for as it deserves. I drives a cab, sir; a four-wheeled cab is what I drives; and a very poor job it is."

"Do you happen to remember a very foggy day about a month ago?"

"Do I not, sir! A reg-ler sneezer that was. Wednesday, the fourteenth of March. I remember the date because I had to pay my bills that morning."

"Will you tell us what happened to you between six and seven in the evening of that day?"

"I will, sir," replied the cabman. "A little before six I was waiting on the arrival side of the Great Northern Station, King's Cross, when I see a gentleman and a lady coming out. The gentleman, he looks up and down, and then he sees me and walks up to the cab and opens the door and helps the lady in. Then he says to me, 'Do you know New Inn?' he says. That's what he says to me what was born and brought up in White Horse Alley, Drury Lane.

" 'Get inside,' says I.

" 'Well,' says he, 'you drive in through the gate in Wych Street' he says, as if he expected me to go in by Houghton Street and down the steps, 'and then,' he says, 'you drive nearly to the end and you'll see a house with a large brass plate at the corner of the doorway. That's where we want to be set down,' he says. And with that he nips in and pulls up the windows and off we goes.

"It took us a full half-hour to get to New Inn through the fog, for I had to get down and lead the horse part of the way. As I drove in under the archway, I saw it was half past six by the clock in the porter's lodge. I drove down nearly to the end of the inn and drew up opposite a house where there was a big brass plate by the doorway. It was Number 31. Then the gent crawls out and pays me, and then he helps the lady out, and away they waddles to the doorway and I see them start up the stairs very slow—reg-ler Pilgrim's Progress. And that was the last I seen of 'em."

Thorndyke wrote down the cabman's statement verbatim together with his own questions, and then asked, "Can you give us any description of the gentleman?"

"The gent," said Wilkins, "was a very respectable looking gent. He knew what was the proper fare for a foggy evening, which is more than some of 'em do. He was a elderly gent about sixty, and he wore spectacles, but he didn't seem to be able to see much through 'em. He was a funny 'un to look at, as round in the back as a turtle, and he walked with his head stuck forward like a goose."

"And the lady; what was she like?"

"I couldn't see much of her because her head was wrapped up in a sort of woolen veil, but I should say she wasn't a chicken. Might have been about the same age as the gent, but I couldn't swear to that. She seemed a trifle rickety on the pins; in fact they were an odd-looking couple. I watched 'em tottering across the pavement and up the stairs hanging on to each other. He was peering through his blinkers, and she was trying to see through her veil. I thought it was jolly good that they'd got a nice sound cab and a steady driver to bring 'em safe home."

"How was the lady dressed?"

"Can't rightly say, not being a hexpert. Her head was done up in this here veil, and she had a small hat on. She had a dark brown mantle with a fringe of beads round it and a black dress, and I noticed when she got into the cab at the station that one of her stockings looked like the bellows of a concertina. That's all I can tell you."

Thorndyke wrote down the last answer and, having read the entire statement aloud, handed the pen to our visitor.

"If that is all correct," he said, "I will ask you to sign your name at the bottom."

"Do you want me to swear a affidavy that it's all true?" asked Wilkins.

"No, thank you," replied Thorndyke. "We may have to call you to give evidence in court, and then you'll be sworn, and you'll also be paid for your attendance. For the present I want you to keep your own counsel and say nothing to anybody about having been here. We have to make some other inquiries, and we don't want the affair talked about."

"I see, sir," said Wilkins, as he laboriously traced his signature at the foot of the statement. "All right, sir; you can depend on me."

"Thank you, Wilkins," said Thorndyke. "And now what are we to give you for your trouble in coming here?"

"I'll leave the fare to you, sir. You know what the information's worth."

Thorndyke laid on the table a couple of coins, at the sight of which the cabman's eyes glistened.

"We have your address, Wilkins," said he. "If we want you as a witness we shall let you know, and if not, there will be more cash for you at the end of a fortnight, provided you have not let this little interview leak out."

Wilkins gathered up the spoils gleefully. "You can trust me, sir," said he, "for to keep my mouth shut. I knows which side my bread's buttered. Good night, gentlemen all."

With this comprehensive salute he moved towards the door and let himself out.

"Well, Jervis; what do you think of it?" Thorndyke asked, as the cabman's footsteps faded away in a creaky diminuendo.

"I don't know what to think. This woman is a new factor in the case, and I don't know how to place her."

"Not entirely new," said Thorndyke. "You have not forgotten those beads that we found in Jeffrey's bedroom, have you?"

"No, I had not forgotten them, but I did not see that they told us much except that some woman had apparently been in his bedroom at some time."

"That, I think, is all that they did tell us. But now they tell us that a particular woman was in his bedroom at a particular time, which is a good deal more significant."

"Yes. It almost looks as if she must have been there when he made away with himself."

"It does, very much."

"The cabman's evidence tells us only that this woman entered the house. The beads tell us that she was in the bedroom; which, as you say, seems to connect her to some extent with Jeffrey's death. It is only a suggestion, but a rather strong suggestion under the peculiar circumstances."

"Even so," said I, "this new fact seems to me so far from clearing up the mystery, only to add to it a fresh element of still deeper mystery."

"I don't see where this woman comes in. It is obvious that her presence at the inn and especially in the bedroom on this occasion and in these strange, secret circumstances, has a rather sinister look, yet I do not see in what way she could have been connected with the tragedy. Do you know who the woman was?" I asked.

"No, I don't know," he replied. "I have a rather strong suspicion that I can identify her, but I am waiting for some further facts."

"Is your suspicion founded on some new matter that you have discovered, or is it deducible from facts that are known to me?"

"I think," he replied, "that you know practically all that I know, although I have, in one instance, turned a very strong suspicion into a certainty by further inquiries. But I think you ought to be able to form some idea as to who this lady probably was."

"But no woman has been mentioned in the case at all."

"No; but I think you should be able to give this lady a name, notwithstanding."

"Should I? Then I begin to suspect that I am not cut out for medicolegal practice, for I don't see the faintest glimmer of a suggestion."

Thorndyke smiled benevolently. "Don't be discouraged, Jervis," said he. "I expect that when you first began to go around the wards, you doubted whether you were cut out for medical practice. I did. For special work one needs special knowledge and an acquired faculty for making use of it. The experienced physician can make a complete diagnosis without any examination at all merely from hearing the patient speak or cough. He has the same facts as a student, but he has acquired the faculty of instantly connecting an abnormality of function with its correlated anatomical change. It is a matter of experience. And with your previous training you will soon acquire the faculty. Try to observe everything. Let nothing escape you. And try constantly to find some connection between facts and events that seem to be unconnected. That is my advice to you; and with that we will put away the Blackmore case for the present and consider our day's work at an end."

CHAPTER 14
THORNDYKE LAYS THE MINE

The information supplied by Mr. Samuel Wilkins, so far from dispelling the cloud of mystery that hung over the Blackmore case, only enveloped it in deeper obscurity, as far as I was concerned. The new problem that Thorndyke offered for a solution was a tougher one than any of the others. He proposed that I should identify and give a name to this mysterious woman. But how could I? No woman, except Mrs. Wilson, had been mentioned in connection with the case. This new person had appeared suddenly from nowhere and straightway vanished without leaving a trace, except for the two or three beads that we had picked up in Jeffrey's room.

Nor was it in the least clear what part, if any, she had played in the tragedy.

A couple of days passed, during which Thorndyke made no further reference to the case. He was away from home most of the time, though how he was engaged I had no idea. What was rather more unusual was that Polton seemed to have deserted the laboratory and taken to outdoor pursuits. I assumed that he had seized the opportunity of leaving me in charge, and I dimly surmised that he was acting as Thorndyke's private agent, as he seemed to have done in the case of Samuel Wilkins.

On the evening of the second day Thornyke came home in obviously good spirits. Therefore I watched him with lively interest.

"I have come to the completion of the Blackmore case. I am just going to write to Marchmont advising him to enter a caveat."

"Do you mean to say that you have discovered a flaw in the will after all?"

"A flaw!" he exclaimed. "My dear Jervis, that second will is a forgery."

I stared at him in amazement, for his assertion sounded like nothing more or less than arrant nonsense.

"But the thing is impossible, Thorndyke," I said. "Not only did the witnesses recognize their own signatures and the painter's greasy fingerprints, but they had both read the will and remembered its contents."

"Yes; that is the interesting feature in the case. It is a very pretty problem. I shall give you one last chance to solve it. Tomorrow evening we shall have to give a full explanation, so you have another twenty-four hours in which to think it over. And meanwhile, I am going to take you to my club to dine. I think we shall be pretty safe there from Mrs. Schallibaum."

He sat down and wrote a letter—apparently quite a short one—and having addressed and stamped it, prepared to go out.

"Come," said he, "let us away. We will lay this mine in the Fleet Street mailbox. I should like to be in Marchmont's office when it explodes."

"I expect," said I, "that the explosion will be felt pretty distinctly in these chambers."

"I expect so too," replied Thorndyke, "and that reminds me that I shall be out all day tomorrow, so if Marchmont calls, you must do all that you can to persuade him to come around after dinner and bring Stephen Blackmore, if possible. I am anxious to have Stephen here, as he will be able to give us some further information and confirm certain matters of fact."

I promised to exercise my utmost powers of persuasion on Mr. Marchmont, which I should certainly have done on my own account, being now on the very tiptoe of curiosity to hear Thorndyke's explanation of the unthinkable conclusion at which he had arrived. The subject dropped completely; nor could I, during the rest of the evening, induce my colleague to reopen it even in the most indirect or allusive manner.

Our expectations of Mr. Marchmont were fully realized, for on the following morning within an hour of Thorndyke's departure from our chambers, the knocker was plied with more than usual emphasis, and I discovered the solicitor in company of an older gentleman. Mr. Marchmont appeared somewhat out of humor, while his companion was obviously in a state of extreme irritation.

"How d'you do, Dr. Jervis?" said Marchmont as he entered at my invitation. "Your friend, I suppose, is not in just now?"

"No. He will not be returning until the evening."

"Hm, I'm sorry. We wished to see him rather particularly. This is my partner, Mr. Winwood."

The latter gentleman bowed stiffly and Marchmont continued, "We have had a letter from Dr. Thorndyke, and it is, I may say, a rather curious letter."

"It is the letter of a madman!" growled Mr. Winwood.

"No, no, Winwood. Nothing of the kind. Control yourself, I beg you. But really, the letter is rather incomprehensible. It relates to the will of the late Jeffrey Blackmore. You know the main facts of the case, and we cannot reconcile it with those facts."

"This is the letter," exclaimed Mr. Winwood, dragging the document from his wallet and slapping it down on the table. "If you are acquainted with the case, sir, just read that, and let us hear what you think."

I took up the letter and read aloud:

"Dear Mr. Marchmont,

"I have gone into the Blackmore case with great care and have now no doubt that the second will is a forgery. Criminal proceedings will, I think, be inevitable, but meanwhile it would be wise to enter a caveat.

"If you could look in at my chambers tomorrow evening, we could talk the case over. I should be glad if you could bring Mr. Stephen Blackmore, whose personal knowledge of the events and the parties concerned would be of great assistance in clearing up obscure details.

"I am, yours sincerely,

"John Evelyn Thorndyke"

"Well!" exclaimed Mr. Winwood, glaring ferociously at me, "what do you think of the learned counsel's opinion?"

"I knew that Thorndyke was writing to you to this effect," I replied, "but I must frankly confess that I can make nothing of it. Have you acted on his advice?"

"Certainly not!" shouted the irascible lawyer. "Do you suppose that we wish to make ourselves the laughingstock of the courts? The thing is impossible—ridiculously impossible!"

"It can't be that, you know," I said, a little stiffly, for I was somewhat nettled by Mr. Winwood's manner, "or Thorndyke would not have written this letter. The conclusion looks as impossible to me as it does to you, but I have complete confidence in Thorndyke. If he says that the will is a forgery, I have no doubt that it is a forgery."

"But how can it be?" roared Winwood. "You know the circumstances under which the will was executed."

"Yes, but so does Thorndyke. And he is not a man who overlooks important facts. It is useless to argue with me. You had better come in this evening and talk it over with him as he suggests."

"It is very inconvenient," grumbled Mr. Winwood. "We shall have to dine in town."

"Yes," said Marchmont, "but it is the only thing to be done. As Dr. Jervis says, we must take it that Thorndyke has something solid to base his opinion on. He doesn't make elementary mistakes. And of course, if what he says is correct, Mr. Stephen's position is totally changed."

"Bah!" exclaimed Winwood, "he has found a hoax, I tell you. The explanation should be worth hearing."

"You mustn't mind Winwood," said Marchmont in an apologetic undertone. "He's a peppery old fellow with a rough tongue, but he doesn't mean any harm." At which statement Winwood assented to—or dissented from, for it was impossible to say which—by a prolonged growl.

"We shall expect you then," I said, "about eight tonight, and you will try to bring Mr. Stephen with you?"

"Yes," replied Marchmont; "I think we can promise that he shall come with us. I have sent him a telegram asking him to attend."

With this the two lawyers took their departure, leaving me to meditate upon my colleague's astonishing statement. That Thorndyke would be able to justify the opinion that he had given, I had no doubt whatever, but yet there was no denying that his proposition was a staggerer.

When Thorndyke returned, I informed him of the visit of our two friends and acquainted him with the sentiments that they had expressed. He smiled with quiet amusement.

"I thought," he remarked, "that letter would bring Marchmont to our door before long. As to Winwood, I have never met him, but I gather that he is one of those people whom you 'mustn't mind.' In a general way, I object to people who tacitly claim exemption from the ordinary rules of conduct that are held to be binding on their fellows. But we will make the best of him and give him a run for his money."

Here Thorndyke smiled mischievously—I understood the meaning of that smile later in the evening—and asked, "What do you think of the affair yourself?"

"I have given it up," I answered. "To my paralyzed brain, the Blackmore case is like an endless algebraical problem propounded by an insane mathematician."

Thorndyke laughed at my comparison, which I flatter myself was a rather apt one.

"Come and dine," said he, "that our hearts may not turn to water under the frown of the disdainful Winwood."

Thereupon we set forth, and after a week's close imprisonment, I once more looked upon the friendly London streets, the cheerfully lighted shop windows and the multitudes of companionable strangers who moved along the pavements.

CHAPTER 15

THORNDYKE EXPLODES THE MINE

We had not been back in our chambers more than a few minutes when the brass knocker on the inner door rattled out its summons. Thorndyke himself opened the door and admitted our three expected visitors.

Marchmont's manner was a bit uneasy. "This is my partner, Mr. Winwood; you haven't met before, I think. We thought we should like to hear some further particulars from you, as we could not quite understand your letter."

"My conclusion, I suppose," said Thorndyke, "was a little unexpected?"

"It was more than that, sir!" exclaimed Winwood. "It was absolutely irreconcilable either with the facts of the case or with common physical possibilities."

"At first glance," Thorndyke agreed, "it would probably have that appearance."

"It has that appearance still to me," said Winwood, growing suddenly red and wrathful, "and I may say that I speak as a solicitor who was practicing law when you were an infant in arms. You tell us, sir, that this will is a forgery; this will, which was executed in broad daylight in the presence of two unimpeachable witnesses, who have sworn, not only to their signatures and the contents of the document, but to their very finger marks on the paper. Are those fingerprints forgeries too? Have you examined and tested them?"

"I have not," replied Thorndyke. "The fact is they are of no interest to me, as I am not disputing the witnesses' signatures."

At this Mr. Winwood fairly danced with irritation. "Marchmont!" he exclaimed fiercely, "you know this good gentleman, I believe. Tell me, is he addicted to practical jokes?"

"Now, my dear Winwood," groaned Marchmont, "I pray you—I beg you—to control yourself. No doubt—"

"But confound it," roared Winwood, "you have, yourself, heard him say that the will is a forgery, but that he doesn't dispute the signatures, which," concluded Winwood, banging his fist down on the table, "is utter nonsense."

"May I suggest," interposed Stephen Blackmore, "that we came here to receive Dr. Thorndyke's explanation of his letter. Perhaps it would be better to postpone any comments until we have heard it."

"Undoubtedly, undoubtedly," said Marchmont. "Let me entreat you, Winwood, to listen patiently and refrain from interruption until we have heard our learned friend's exposition of the case."

"Oh, very well," Winwood replied sulkily. "I'll say no more."

He sank into a chair with the manner of a man who shuts himself up and turns the key, and so remained—except when the internal pressure approached bursting point—throughout the subsequent proceedings, silent, stony, and impassive, like a seated statue of obstinacy.

"I take it," said Marchmont, "that you have some new facts that are not in our possession?"

"Yes," replied Thorndyke. "We have some new facts, and we have made some new use of the old ones. But how shall I lay the case before you? Shall I state my theory of the sequence of events and furnish the verification afterwards? Or shall I retrace the actual course of my investigations and give you the facts in the order in which I obtained them myself, with the inferences from them?"

"I almost think," said Mr. Marchmont, "that it would be better if you would put us in possession of the new facts. Then, if the conclusions that follow from them are not sufficiently obvious, we could hear the argument. What do you say, Winwood?"

Mr. Winwood roused himself for an instant, barked out the one word "Facts," and shut himself up again with a snap.

"You would like to have the new facts by themselves?" said Thorndyke.

"If you please. The facts only for now."

"Very well," said Thorndyke, and here I caught his eye with a mischievous twinkle in it that I understood perfectly. I had most of the facts myself and realized how much these two lawyers were likely to extract from them. Winwood was going to "have a run for his money," as Thorndyke had promised.

My colleague, having placed on the table by his side a small cardboard box and the sheets of notes from his file, glanced quickly at Mr. Winwood and began: "The first important new facts came into my possession on the day on which you introduced the case to me. In the evening after you left, I availed myself of Mr. Stephen's kind invitation to look over his uncle's chambers at Number 31, New Inn. I wished to ascertain, if possible, what had been the habits of the deceased during his residence there. When I arrived with Dr. Jervis, Mr.

Stephen was in the chambers, and I learned from him that his uncle was an Oriental scholar and that he had a very thorough acquaintance with the cuneiform writing. Now, while I was talking with Mr. Stephen I made a very curious discovery. On the wall over the fireplace hung a large framed photograph of an ancient inscription in the cuneiform character; and that photograph was upside down."

"Upside down!" exclaimed Stephen. "That is very odd."

"Very odd indeed," agreed Thorndyke, "and very suggestive. The photograph had evidently been in the frame some years but had apparently never been hung up before."

"It had not," said Stephen, "though I don't know how you arrived at the fact. It used to stand on the mantelpiece in his old rooms in Jermyn Street."

"Well," continued Thorndyke, "the frame maker had pasted his label on the back of the frame, and as this label hung the right way up, it appeared as if the person who fixed the photograph on the wall had adopted it as a guide."

"It is very extraordinary," said Stephen. "I should have thought the person who hung it would have asked Uncle Jeffrey which was the right way up; and I can't imagine how on earth it could have hung all those months without his noticing it. He must have been practically blind."

Here Marchmont, who had been thinking hard with knitted brows, suddenly brightened up.

"I see your point," said he. "You mean that if Jeffrey was as blind as that, it would have been possible for some person to substitute a false will, which he might sign without noticing the substitution."

"That wouldn't make the will a forgery," growled Winwood. "If Jeffrey signed it, it was Jeffrey's will. You could contest it if you could prove the fraud. But he said, 'This is my will,' and the two witnesses read it and have identified it."

"Did they read it aloud?" asked Stephen.

"No, they did not," replied Thorndyke.

"Can you prove substitution?" asked Marchmont.

"I haven't asserted it," answered Thorndyke. "My position is that the will is a forgery."

"But it is not," said Winwood.

"We won't argue it now," said Thorndyke. "I ask you to note the fact that the inscription was upside down. I also observed on the walls of the chambers some valuable Japanese color prints on which were recent damp spots. I noted that the sitting room had a gas stove and that the kitchen contained practically no stores or remains of food and hardly any traces of even the simplest cooking. In the bedroom I found a large box that had contained a considerable stock of candles that was now nearly empty. I examined the clothing of the deceased. On the soles of the boots I observed dried mud, which was unlike that on my own and Jervis's boots from the gravelly square of the inn. I noted a crease on each leg of the deceased man's trousers as if they had been turned up halfway to the knee, and in the waistcoat pocket I found the stump of a 'Contango' pencil. On the floor of the bedroom, I found a portion of an oval glass somewhat like that of a watch or locket, but ground at the edge to a double bevel. Dr. Jervis and I also found one or two beads, all of dark brown glass."

Here Thorndyke paused, and Marchmont, who had been gazing at him with growing amazement, said nervously, "Er . . . yes. Very interesting. These observations of yours er . . . are . . ."

"Are all the observations that I made at New Inn."

The two lawyers looked at one another and Stephen Blackmore stared fixedly at a spot on the rug.

Then Mr. Winwood's face contorted itself into a sour, lopsided smile. "You might have observed a good many other things, sir," said he, "if you had looked. If you had examined the doors, you would have noted that they had hinges and were covered with paint; and if you had looked up the chimney, you might have noted that it was black inside."

"Now, now, Winwood," protested Marchmont in an agony of uneasiness as to what his partner might say next, "I must really beg you to refrain from . . . what Mr. Winwood means, Dr. Thorndyke, is that we do not quite perceive the relevancy of these . . . ah . . . observations of yours."

"Probably not," said Thorndyke, "but you will perceive their relevancy later. For the present, I will ask you to note the facts and bear them in mind, so that you may be able to follow the argument when we come to that.

"The next set of data I acquired on the same evening, when Dr. Jervis gave me a detailed account of a very strange adventure that befell him. I need not burden you with all the details, but I will give you the substance of his story."

He then proceeded to recount the incidents connected with my visits to Mr. Graves, dwelling on personal peculiarities of the parties concerned and especially of the patient, and not even forgetting the very singular spectacles worn by Mr. Weiss. He also explained briefly the construction of the chart, presenting the latter for the inspection of his hearers. To this recital our three visitors listened in utter bewilderment, as indeed I also did, for I could not conceive in what way my adventures could possibly be related to the affairs of the late Mr. Blackmore.

This was manifestly the view taken by Mr. Marchmont, for during a pause in which the chart was handed to him, he remarked somewhat stiffly, "I am assuming, Dr. Thorndyke, that the curious story you are telling us has some relevance to the matter in which we are interested."

"You are quite correct in your assumption," replied Thorndyke. "The story is very relevant indeed, as you will presently be convinced."

"Thank you," said Marchmont, sinking back once more into his chair with a sigh of resignation.

"A few days ago," pursued Thorndyke, "Dr. Jervis and I located with the aid of this chart, the house to which he had been called. We found that the late tenant had left somewhat hurriedly and that the house was for rent. As no other kind of investigation was possible, we obtained the keys and made an exploration of the premises."

Here he gave a brief account of our visit and the conditions that we observed, and was proceeding to furnish a list of the articles that we had found under the grate, when Mr. Winwood started from his chair.

"Really, sir!" he exclaimed, "this is too much! Have I come here, at great personal inconvenience, to hear you read the inventory of a dust heap?"

Thorndyke smiled benevolently and caught my eye once more with a gleam of amusement.

"Sit down, Mr. Winwood," he said quietly. "You came here to learn the facts of the case, and I am giving them to you. Please don't interrupt needlessly and waste time."

Winwood stared at him ferociously for several seconds, then somewhat disconcerted by the unruffled calm of his manner, he uttered a snort of defiance, sat down heavily and shut himself up again.

"We will now," Thorndyke continued, with unmoved serenity, "consider these relics in more detail, and we will begin with this pair of spectacles. They belonged to a person who was near-sighted and astigmatic in the left eye and almost certainly blind in the right. Such a description agrees entirely with Dr. Jervis's account of the sick man."

He paused for a moment, and then as no one made any comment, proceeded: "We next come to these little pieces of reed, which you, Mr. Stephen, will probably recognize as the remains of a Japanese brush, such as is used for writing in Chinese ink or for making small drawings."

Again he paused as though expecting some remark from his listeners, but no one spoke, and he continued. "Then there is this bottle with the theatrical wig maker's label on it, which once contained cement such as is used for fixing on false beards, moustaches or eyebrows."

He paused once more and looked round expectantly at his audience, none of whom, however, volunteered any remark.

"Do none of these objects that I have described and shown you seem to have any significance for us?" he asked, in a tone of some surprise.

"They convey nothing to me," said Mr. Marchmont, glancing at his partner, who shook his head like a restive horse.

"Nor to you, Mr. Stephen?"

"No," replied Stephen. "Under the existing circumstances they convey no reasonable suggestion to me."

Thorndyke hesitated as if he were half inclined to say something more; then with a slight shrug, he turned over his notes and resumed. "The next group of new facts is concerned with the signatures of the recent checks. We have photographed them and placed them together for the purpose of comparison and analysis."

"I am not prepared to question the signatures," said Winwood. "We have had a highly expert opinion, which would override ours in a court of law even if we differed from it; which I think we do not."

"Yes," said Marchmont, "that is so. I think we must accept the signatures, especially as that of the will has been proved beyond any question, to be authentic."

"Very well," agreed Thorndyke, "we will pass over the signatures. Then we have some further evidence in regard to the spectacles, which serves to verify our conclusions respecting them."

"Perhaps," said Marchmont, "we might pass over that too, as we do not seem to have reached any conclusions."

"As you please," said Thorndyke. "It is important, but we can reserve it for verification. The next item will interest you more, I think. It is the signed and witnessed statement of

Samuel Wilkins, the driver of the cab in which the deceased came home to the inn on the evening of his death."

My colleague was right. An actual document, signed by a tangible witness, who could be put in the box and sworn, brought both lawyers to a state of attention. When Thorndyke read out the cabman's evidence, their attention soon quickened into undisguised astonishment.

"But this is a most mysterious affair," exclaimed Marchmont. "Who could this woman have been, and what could she have been doing in Jeffrey's chambers at this time? Can you throw any light on it, Mr. Stephen?"

"It is a complete mystery to me," replied Stephen. "My uncle Jeffrey was a confirmed old bachelor, and although he did not dislike women, he was far from partial to their society, wrapped up as he was in his favorite studies. To the best of my belief, he had not a single female friend. He was not on intimate terms even with his sister, Mrs. Wilson."

"Very remarkable," mused Marchmont. "Most remarkable. But perhaps you can tell us, Dr. Thorndyke, who this woman was?"

"I think," replied Thorndyke, "that the next item of evidence will enable you to form an opinion for yourselves. I only obtained it yesterday, and as it made my case quite complete, I wrote off to you immediately. It is the statement of Joseph Ridley, another cabman, and unfortunately a rather unobservant fellow, unlike Wilkins. He has not much to tell us, but what little he has is highly instructive. Here is the statement, signed by the deponent and witnessed by me.

'My name is Joseph Ridley. I am the driver of a four-wheeled cab. On the fourteenth of March, the day of the great fog, I was waiting at Vauxhall Station, where I had just set down a fare. About five o'clock a lady came and told me to drive over to Upper Kennington Lane to take up a passenger. She was a middle-sized woman. I could not tell what her age was, or what she was like, because her head was wrapped up in a sort of knitted, woolen veil to keep out the fog. I did not notice how she was dressed. She got into the cab, and I led the horse over to Upper Kennington Lane and a little way up the lane, until the lady tapped at the front window for me to stop.

'She got out of the cab and told me to wait. Then she went away and disappeared in the fog. Presently a lady and gentleman came from the direction in which she had gone. The lady looked like the same lady, but I won't answer to that. Her head was wrapped up in the same kind of veil, and I noticed that she had on a dark colored mantle with bead fringe on it.

'The gentleman was clean shaved and wore spectacles, and he stooped a good deal. I can't say whether his sight was good or bad. He helped the lady into the cab and told me to drive to the Great Northern Station, King's Cross. Then he got in himself, and I drove off. I got to the station about a quarter to six, and the lady and gentleman got out. The gentleman paid my fare, and they both went into the station. I did not notice anything unusual about either of them. Directly after they had gone, I got a fresh fare and drove away.'

"That," Thorndyke concluded, "is Joseph Ridley's statement, and I think it will enable you to give a meaning to the other facts that I have offered for your consideration."

"I am not so sure about that," said Marchmont. "It is all exceedingly mysterious. Your suggestion is, of course, that the woman who came to New Inn in the cab was Mrs. Schallibaum?"

"Not at all," replied Thorndyke. "My suggestion is that the woman was Jeffrey Blackmore."

There was a deathly silence for a few moments. We were all absolutely thunderstruck, and sat gaping at Thorndyke in speechless astonishment. Then Mr. Winwood fairly bounced out of his chair.

"But—my—good—sir!" he screeched. "Jeffrey Blackmore was with her at the time!"

"Naturally," replied Thorndyke, "my suggestion implies that the person who was with her was not Jeffrey Blackmore."

"But he was!" bawled Winwood. "The porter saw him!"

"The porter saw a person whom he believed to be Jeffrey Blackmore. I suggest that the porter's belief was erroneous."

"Well," snapped Winwood, "perhaps you can prove that it was. I don't see how you are going to, but perhaps you can."

He subsided once more into his chair and glared defiantly at Thorndyke.

"You seemed," said Stephen, "to suggest some connection between the sick man, Graves, and my uncle. I noted it at the time, but put it aside as impossible. Was I right? Did you mean to suggest any connection?"

"I suggest something more than a connection. I suggest identity. My position is that the sick man, Graves, was your uncle."

"From Dr. Jervis's description," said Stephen, "this man must have been very like my uncle. Both were blind in the right eye and had very poor vision with the left, and my uncle certainly used brushes of the kind that you have shown us when writing in the Japanese character, for I have watched him and admired his skill. But—"

"But," said Marchmont, "there is the insurmountable objection that at the very time when this man was lying sick in Kennington Lane, Mr. Jeffrey was living at New Inn."

"What evidence is there of that?" asked Thorndyke.

"Evidence!" Marchmont exclaimed impatiently. "Why, my dear sir—"

He paused suddenly, and, leaning forward, regarded Thorndyke with a new and rather startled expression. "You mean to suggest . . ." he began.

"I suggest that Jeffrey Blackmore never lived at New Inn at all."

For the moment, Marchmont seemed absolutely paralyzed by astonishment.

"This is an amazing proposition!" he exclaimed at length. "Yet the thing is certainly not impossible, for now that you recall the fact, I realize that no one who had known him previously—excepting his brother, John—ever saw him at the inn. The question of identity was never raised."

"Except," said Mr. Winwood, "in regard to the body, which was certainly that of Jeffrey Blackmore."

"Yes, yes. Of course," said Marchmont. "I had forgotten that for the moment. The body was identified beyond doubt. You don't dispute the identity of the body, do you?"

"Certainly not," replied Thorndyke.

Here Mr. Winwood grasped his hair with both hands and stuck his elbows on his knees, while Marchmont drew forth a large handkerchief and mopped his forehead. Stephen Blackmore looked from one to the other expectantly, and finally said, "If I might make a suggestion, it would be that, as Dr. Thorndyke has now shown us the pieces of the puzzle, he should be so kind as to put them together for our information."

"Yes," agreed Marchmont, "that will be the best plan. Let us have the argument, Doctor, and any additional evidence that you possess."

"The argument," said Thorndyke, "will be a rather long one, as the facts are so numerous, and there are some points in verification on which I shall have to dwell in some detail. We will have some coffee to clear our brains first."

CHAPTER 16

AN EXPOSITION

"You may have wondered," Thorndyke commenced, when he had poured the coffee, "what induced me to undertake the minute investigation of so apparently simple and straightforward a case. Perhaps I had better explain that first and let you see what was the real starting point of the inquiry.

"When you, Mr. Marchmont and Mr. Stephen, introduced the case to me, I made a very brief summary of the facts as you presented them, and one or two immediately attracted my attention. In the first place, there was the will. It contained no new matter; it expressed no changed intentions; it met no new circumstances. In short it was not really a new will at all, but merely a repetition of the first one, drafted in different and less suitable language. It created the possibility that, in certain circumstances, John Blackmore might become the beneficiary, contrary to the obvious wishes of the testator.

"The next point that impressed me was the manner of Mrs. Wilson's death. She died of cancer. Now, people do not die suddenly and unexpectedly of cancer. This terrible disease stands almost alone in that it marks out its victim months in advance. A person who has an incurable cancer is a person whose death may be predicted with certainty and its date fixed within comparatively narrow limits.

"And now observe the remarkable series of coincidences: Mrs. Wilson died on the twelfth of March of this present year. Mr. Jeffrey's second will was signed on the twelfth of November of last year, at a time when the existence of cancer must have been known to Mrs. Wilson's doctor, and might have been known to any of her relatives who chose to inquire after her. The remarkable change in Mr. Jeffrey's habits coincides in the most singular way with the same events. The cancer must have been detectable as early as September of last year, about the time when Mrs. Wilson made her will. Mr. Jeffrey went to the inn at the beginning of October. From that time his habits were totally changed, and I can demonstrate to you that a change—not a gradual, but an abrupt change—took place in the character of his signature.

"In short, the whole of this peculiar set of circumstances—the change in Jeffrey's habits, the change in his signature, and the execution of his strange will—came into existence about the time when Mrs. Wilson was first known to be suffering from cancer.

"This struck me as a very suggestive fact.

"Then there is the extraordinarily opportune date of Mr. Jeffrey's death. Mrs. Wilson died on the twelfth of March. Mr. Jeffrey was found dead on the fifteenth of March, having apparently died on the fourteenth on which day he was seen alive. If he had died only three days sooner, he would have predeceased Mrs. Wilson, and her property would never have passed on to him at all; while if he had lived only a day or two longer, he would have learned of her death and would almost certainly have made a new will or codicil in his nephew's favor.

"Circumstances, therefore, conspired in the most singular manner in favor of John Blackmore.

"But there is yet another coincidence. Jeffrey's body was found, by the merest chance, the day after his death. But it might have remained undiscovered for weeks, or even months; and if it had, it would have been impossible to fix the date of his death. Then Mrs. Wilson's next of kin would certainly have contested John Blackmore's claim—and probably with success—on the ground that Jeffrey died before Mrs. Wilson. But all this uncertainty is provided for by the circumstance that Mr. Jeffrey paid his rent personally—and prematurely—to the porter on the fourteenth of March, thus establishing beyond question the fact that he was alive on that date. Further, in case the porter's memory should be untrustworthy or his statement doubted, Jeffrey furnished a signed and dated document—the check—which could be produced in court to furnish incontestable proof of survival.

"To sum up this part of the evidence. Here was a will that enabled John Blackmore to inherit the fortune of a man who almost certainly had no intention of bequeathing it to him. The wording of the will and the time, the manner, and the circumstances of the testator's death, all seemed to be precisely adjusted to the fact that the approximate date of Mrs. Wilson's death was known some months before it occurred.

"Now you must admit that this compound group of coincidences, all conspiring to a single end—the enrichment of John Blackmore—has a very singular appearance. Coincidences are common enough in real life, but we cannot accept too many at a time. My feeling was that there were too many in this case and that I could not accept them without a searching inquiry."

Thorndyke paused, and Mr. Marchmont, who had listened with close attention, nodded, as he glanced at his silent partner. "You have stated the case with remarkable clearness," he said, "and I am free to confess that some of the points that you have raised had escaped my notice."

"My first idea," Thorndyke resumed, "was that John Blackmore, taking advantage of the mental enfeeblement produced by the opium habit, had dictated this will to Jeffrey. It was then that I sought permission to inspect Jeffrey's chambers to learn what I could about him and to see for myself whether they presented the dirty and disorderly appearance characteristic of opium use. But when I thought over the case, it seemed to me that this explanation hardly met the facts. Looking over my notes I observed two points that seemed worth considering. One was that neither of the witnesses to the will was really acquainted with Jeffrey Blackmore, both being strangers who had accepted his identity on his own statement. The other was that no one who had previously known him, with the single exception of his brother John, had ever seen Jeffrey at the inn.

"What was the import of these two facts? They suggested the desirability of considering the question: Was the person who signed the will really Jeffrey Blackmore? The contrary supposition—that someone had personated Jeffrey and forged his signature to a false will—seemed wildly improbable. I did not, however, for a moment, think that this was the true explanation, but I resolved to bear it in mind, to test it when the opportunity arose, and consider it by the light of any fresh facts that I might acquire.

"The new facts came sooner than I had expected. That same evening I went with Dr. Jervis to New Inn and found Mr. Stephen in the chambers. He informed me that Jeffrey was a learned Orientalist with an expert knowledge of cuneiform writing. Yet even as he was telling me this, I looked over his shoulder and saw a cuneiform inscription hanging on the wall upside down.

"Now, there could be only one reasonable explanation. Disregarding the fact that no one would screw the suspension plates on a frame without ascertaining which was the right way up, and assuming it to be hung up inverted, it was impossible that the misplacement could have been overlooked by Jeffrey. He was not blind, though his sight was defective. The frame was thirty inches long and the individual characters were nearly an inch in length. There was, I repeat, only one reasonable explanation, which was that the person who had inhabited those chambers was not Jeffrey Blackmore.

"This conclusion received considerable support from a fact which I observed later, but mention now. On examining the soles of the shoes taken from the dead man's feet, I found only the ordinary mud of the streets. There was no trace of the peculiar gravelly mud that adhered to my own boots and Jervis's, and which came from the square of the inn. Yet the porter distinctly stated that the deceased, after paying the rent, walked back towards his chambers across the square. The mud should, therefore, have been conspicuous on his shoes.

"And so, a wildly speculative hypothesis had assumed a high degree of probability.

"When Mr. Stephen was gone, Jervis and I looked over the chambers thoroughly, and another curious fact came to light. On the wall were a number of fine Japanese prints, all of which showed recent damp spots. How came they to be damp? There was a gas stove in the room, and a gas stove has at least the virtue of preserving a dry atmosphere. It was winter weather when the stove would naturally be pretty constantly alight. How came the walls to be so damp? The answer seemed to be that the stove had been lighted only occasionally. This suggestion was borne out by a further examination of the rooms. The kitchen had practically no food and hardly any arrangements even for simple bachelor cooking. The bedroom offered the same suggestion. The soap in the washstand was shriveled and cracked. There was no castoff linen. The shirts in the drawers, though clean, had the peculiar yellowish, faded appearance that linen acquires when long out of use. In short, the rooms had the appearance of not having been lived in at all, but only visited at intervals.

"Against this view, however, was the statement of the night porter that he had often seen a light in Jeffrey's sitting room at one o'clock in the morning, with the apparent implication that it was then turned out. Now a light may be left in an empty room, but its extinction implies the presence of some person to extinguish it; unless some automatic device be adopted for putting it out at a given time. Such a device—the alarm movement of a clock, for instance, with a suitable attachment—is a simple enough matter, but my search of the rooms failed to discover anything of the kind. However, when looking over the drawers in the bedroom, I came upon a large box that had held a considerable quantity of candles. There were only a few left, but a flat candlestick with numerous wick ends in its socket accounted for the remainder.

"These candles seemed to dispose of the difficulty. They were not necessary for ordinary lighting, since gas was on in all three rooms. For what purpose, then, were they used? I subsequently obtained some of the same brand candles and experimented with them. Each candle was seven and a quarter inches in length, and I found that they burned in still air at the rate of a fraction over one inch in an hour. We may say that one of these candles would burn in still air a little over six hours. It would thus be possible for the person who inhabited these rooms to go away at seven o'clock in the evening and leave a light, which would burn until past one in the morning and then extinguish itself. This, of course, was only a theory, but it destroyed the significance of the night porter's statement.

"But, if the person who inhabited these chambers was not Jeffrey, who was he?

"The answer to that question seemed plain enough. There was only one person who had a strong motive for perpetrating a fraud of this kind, and there was only one person to whom it was possible. If this person was not Jeffrey, he must have been very like Jeffrey. The only person who fulfils the conditions is John Blackmore.

"We have learned from Mr. Stephen that John and Jeffrey, though very different in appearance in later years, were much alike as young men. But when two brothers who are much alike as young men, become unlike in later life, we often find that the differences are superficial and that the essential likeness remains. Thus, in the present case, Jeffrey was clean-shaven, had bad eyesight, wore spectacles, and stooped as he walked; John wore a beard and moustache, had good eyesight, did not wear spectacles, and had a brisk gait and upright carriage. But supposing John to shave off his beard and moustache, to put on spectacles, and to stoop in his walk, these conspicuous but superficial differences would vanish and the original likeness reappear.

"There is another consideration. John had been an actor—an actor of some experience. Now any person can, with some care and practice, make up a disguise; the great difficulty is to support that disguise by a suitable manner and voice. But to an experienced actor this difficulty does not exist. To him, impersonation is easy; and, moreover, an actor is precisely the person to whom the idea of disguise would occur.

"There is a small item bearing on this point, so small as to be hardly worth calling evidence, but just worth noting. In the pocket of the waistcoat taken from the body of Jeffrey, I found the stump of a 'Contango' pencil; a pencil that is sold for the use of stock dealers and brokers. Now John was an outside broker and might very probably have used such a pencil, whereas Jeffrey had no connection with the stock markets, and there is no reason why he should have possessed a pencil of this kind. But the fact is merely suggestive; it has no evidential value.

"A more important inference is to be drawn from all of the collected signatures. The change in the signature occurred abruptly. There are two distinct forms with no intermediate varieties. In itself this is suspicious. But a remark made by Mr. Britton furnishes a valuable piece of evidence on this point. He admitted that the character of the signature had undergone a change, but observed that the change did not affect the individual or personal character of the writing. This is very important; for handwriting is, as it were, an extension of the personality of the writer. And just as a man to some extent shares his personality with his near blood relations in the form of family resemblance, so his handwriting often shows a subtle likeness to that of his near relatives. The inference, then, is that if the signature of the will was forged, it was probably forged by a relative of the deceased. But the only relative in question is his brother John.

"All the facts, therefore, pointed to John Blackmore as the person who occupied these chambers, and I accordingly adopted that view as a working hypothesis."

"But this was all pure speculation," objected Mr. Winwood.

"Not speculation," said Thorndyke. "Hypothesis. It was ordinary inductive reasoning such as we employ in scientific research. I started with the purely tentative hypothesis that the person who signed the will was not Jeffrey Blackmore.

"I assumed this, and accordingly I tested it with each new fact. As each new fact said 'Yes,' and no fact said definitely 'No,' its probability increased rapidly. It is a perfectly sound method, for one knows that if a hypothesis be true, it will lead sooner or later to a crucial fact by which its truth can be demonstrated.

"To resume our argument. We have now set up the proposition that John Blackmore was the tenant of Number 31, New Inn and that he was impersonating Jeffrey.

"If the tenant of New Inn was John, then Jeffrey must be elsewhere, since his concealment at the inn was clearly impossible. He could not have been far away, for he had to be producible at short notice whenever Mrs. Wilson died. But if he was producible, he must have been in the control of John. He could not have been at large, for that would have involved the danger of his being seen and recognized. He could not have been in any institution or place where he would be in contact with strangers, so he must be in some sort of confinement. But it is difficult to keep an adult in confinement in an ordinary house. So what alternative method could be suggested?

"The most obvious method is that of keeping the prisoner in such a state of debility as would confine him to his bed. But such debility could be produced only by starvation, unsuitable food, or chronic poisoning. Of these alternatives, poisoning is much more exact, more calculable in its effect, and more under control. The probabilities, then, were in favor of chronic poisoning.

"Having reached this stage, I recalled a singular case which Jervis had mentioned to me and which seemed to illustrate this method. On our return home I asked him for further particulars, and he then gave me a very detailed description of the patient and the circumstances. The upshot was rather startling. I had looked on his case as merely illustrative. But when I had heard his account, I began to suspect that there was something more than mere parallelism of method. It began to look as if his patient, Mr. Graves, might actually be Jeffrey Blackmore.

"The coincidences were remarkable. The general appearance of the patient tallied completely with Mr. Stephen's description of his uncle Jeffrey. The mystery patient had a tremulous iris in his right eye and had clearly suffered from dislocation of the lens. From Mr. Stephen's account of his uncle's loss of sight in the right eye after a fall, I judged that Jeffrey had also suffered from dislocation of the lens and therefore had a tremulous iris in the right eye. The patient, Graves, evidently had defective vision in his left eye, as proved by the marks made behind his ears by his spectacles. But Jeffrey had defective vision in his left eye and wore spectacles as well. Lastly, the patient, Graves, was suffering from chronic morphine poisoning, and morphine was found in the body of Jeffrey.

"Once more, it appeared to me that there were too many coincidences.

"The question as to whether Graves and Jeffrey were identical admitted of fairly easy disproof; for if Graves was still alive, he could not be Jeffrey. It was an important question and

I resolved to test it without delay. That night Jervis and I plotted out the chart, and on the following morning we located the house, but it was empty. The birds had flown, and we failed to discover whither they had gone.

"However, we entered the house and explored. I have told you about the massive bolts and fastenings that we found on the bedroom doors and window, showing that the room had been used as a prison. I have told you of the objects that we picked out of the dust heap under the grate. I need not speak now of the obvious suggestions offered by the Japanese brush and the bottle of 'spirit gum' or cement, but I must trouble you with some details concerning the broken spectacles. For here we had come upon the crucial fact to which as I have said all sound inductive reasoning brings one sooner or later.

"The spectacles were of a rather unique pattern. The right eyepiece was fitted with plain glass, as is usual in the case of a blind or useless eye. It was very much shattered, but its character was obvious. The glass of the left eye was much thicker and fortunately less damaged, so that I was able accurately to test its refraction.

"When I reached home, I laid the pieces of the spectacles together, tested the left eye glass, and wrote down a full description such as would have been given by the surgeon to the spectacle maker. Here it is, and I will ask you to note it carefully.

" 'Spectacles for constant use. Steel frame, curl sides, broad bridge with gold lining. Distance between centers 6.2 centimeters; extreme length of sidebars, 18.3 centimeters.

" 'Right eye plain glass.

" 'Left eye -5.75 D. spherical and -3.25 D. cylindrical, axis 35°'

"The spectacles, you see, were of a very distinctive character and seemed to offer a good chance of identification. The frames are made by only one firm of opticians in London, Parry & Cuxton of Regent Street. I therefore wrote to Mr. Cuxton, who knows me, asking him if he had supplied spectacles to the late Jeffrey Blackmore—here is a copy of my letter—and if so, whether he would mind letting me have a full description of them, together with the name of the oculist who prescribed them.

"He replied in this letter, which is pinned to the copy of mine, that about four years ago, he supplied a pair of glasses to Mr. Jeffrey Blackmore, and described them thus:

" 'The spectacles were for constant use and had steel frames with curl sides, the length of the sidebars including the curled ends being 13.3 cm. The bridge was broad with a gold lining plate. Distance between centers 6.2 cm.

" 'Right eye plain glass.

" 'Left eye −5.75 D. spherical and -3.25 D. cylindrical, axis 35°

" 'The spectacles were prescribed by Mr. Hindley of Wimpole Street.'

"Here, then, we have three important facts. One is that the spectacles found by us at Kennington Lane were undoubtedly Jeffrey's, for it is as unlikely that there exists another pair of spectacles exactly identical with these as that there exists another face exactly like Jeffrey's face. The second fact is that the description of Jeffrey tallies completely with that of the sick man, Graves, as given by Dr. Jervis. The third is that when Jeffrey was seen by Mr. Hindley, there was no sign of his being addicted to the taking of morphine. The first and second facts constitute complete identification."

"Yes," said Marchmont, "I think we must admit the identification is quite conclusive."

"A few days ago I wrote to Mr. Stephen," said Thorndyke, "asking him if he possessed a recent photograph of his Uncle Jeffrey. He had one, and he sent it to me by return mail. Dr. Jervis examined it, without any hint whatever from me, and he identified it as the portrait of the sick man, Graves."

"Indeed!" exclaimed Marchmont. "This is most important. Are you prepared to swear to the identity, Dr. Jervis?"

"I have not the slightest doubt," I replied, "that the portrait is that of Mr. Graves."

"Excellent!" said Marchmont, rubbing his hands gleefully. "This will be much more convincing to a jury. Pray go on, Dr. Thorndyke."

"We had now reached a definite, demonstrable fact; and that fact, as you see, disposed at once of the main question— the genuineness of the will. For if the man at Kennington Lane was Jeffrey Blackmore, then the man at Number 31, New Inn was not. But it was the latter who had signed the will. Therefore the will was not signed by Jeffrey Blackmore. That is to say, it was a forgery. The case was complete for the purposes of the civil proceedings; the rest of my investigations had reference to the criminal prosecution that was inevitable. Shall I proceed, or is your interest confined to the will?"

"I want to hear how you propose to lay hands on the villain who murdered poor old Uncle Jeffrey!" exclaimed Stephen, "for I suppose he did murder him?"

"I think there is no doubt of it," replied Thorndyke.

"Then," said Marchmont, "we will hear the rest of the argument, if you please."

"Very well," said Thorndyke. "As the evidence stands, we have proved that Jeffrey Blackmore was a prisoner in the house in Kennington Lane and that someone was impersonating him at New Inn. That someone, we have seen, was in all probability, John Blackmore. We now have to consider the man Weiss. Who was he and can we connect him in any way with New Inn?

"We may note in passing that Weiss and the coachman were apparently one and the same person. They were never seen together. When Weiss was present, the coachman was not available even for so urgent a service as the obtaining of an antidote to the poison. Weiss always appeared some time after Jervis's arrival and disappeared some time before his departure, in each case sufficiently long to allow of a change of disguise.

"He was clearly heavily disguised, as we see by his unwillingness to show himself even by the light of a candle. But there is an item of positive evidence on this point that is important. It is furnished by the spectacles worn by Weiss, of which you have heard Jervis's description. These spectacles had very peculiar optical properties. When you looked through them they had the properties of plain glass; when you looked at them they had the appearance of lenses. But only one kind of glass possesses these properties; namely, that which like an ordinary watch crystal has curved, parallel surfaces. But why would a person wear watch crystal spectacles? Clearly, not to assist his vision. The only alternative is disguise.

"The impersonator is therefore in this dilemma: if he wears actual spectacles, he cannot see through them; if he wears false spectacles of plain glass, his disguise will probably be detected. There is only one way out of the difficulty, and that not a very satisfactory one, but Mr. Weiss seems to have adopted it in lieu of a better. It is that of using watch crystal spectacles such as I have described.

"The importance of this conclusion emerges. They were not merely peculiar spectacles; they were unique. It is exceedingly likely that there is not in the entire world another similar pair of spectacles, and so the finding of these fragments of glass in the bedroom establishes a considerable probability that Mr. Weiss was at some time in the chambers at New Inn.

"And now let us gather up the threads of this part of the argument. We are inquiring into the identity of the man Weiss.

"In the first place, we find him committing a secret crime from which John Blackmore alone will benefit. This suggests the probability that he was John Blackmore.

"Then we find that he was a man of normal eyesight who was wearing spectacles for the purpose of disguise.

"John Blackmore did not reside at New Inn, but at some place within easy reach of it. And Weiss resided at a place within easy reach of New Inn.

"John Blackmore must have had possession and control of the person of Jeffrey. And Weiss had possession and control of the person of Jeffrey.

"Weiss wore spectacles of a certain peculiar and probably unique character. And portions of such spectacles were found in the chambers at New Inn.

"The overwhelming probability, therefore, is that Weiss and the tenant of New Inn were one and the same person and that that person was John Blackmore."

"That," said Mr. Winwood, "is a very plausible argument. But you observe, sir, that yet one problem remains."

Thorndyke smiled genially. I think he forgave Winwood everything for that remark.

"You are quite right, sir," he said. "It does. And for that reason the demonstration is not absolute. We have now furnished fairly conclusive evidence on three heads: we have proved that the sick man, Graves, was Jeffrey Blackmore; that the tenant of New Inn was John Blackmore; and that the man Weiss was also John Blackmore. The final problem is this: we now have to prove that John and Jeffrey were together in the chambers at New Inn on the night of Jeffrey's death.

"We know that two persons and two persons only came from Kennington Lane to New Inn. One of those persons was the tenant of New Inn—that is, John Blackmore. Who was the other? Jeffrey is known by us to have been at Kennington Lane. His body was found on the following morning in the room at New Inn. No third person is known to have come from Kennington Lane; no third person is known to have arrived at New Inn. The inference, by exclusion, is that the second person—the woman—was Jeffrey.

An Exposition

"Again, Jeffrey had to be brought from Kennington to the inn by John. But John was impersonating Jeffrey and was made up to resemble him very closely. Therefore Jeffrey would have to be disguised in some way, and what disguise could be simpler and more effective than the one that I suggest was used?

"It was unavoidable that the cabman should know that Jeffrey was not alone when he came to the inn that night. Had it become known that a man had accompanied him to his chambers, some suspicion might have arisen, and that suspicion would have pointed to John. But if it had transpired that Jeffrey was accompanied by a woman, there would have been less suspicion, and that suspicion would not have pointed to John Blackmore.

"Thus all the general probabilities are in favor of the hypothesis that this woman was Jeffrey Blackmore. There is, however, an item of positive evidence that strongly supports this view. When I examined the clothing of the deceased, I found on the trousers a horizontal crease on each leg as if the trousers had been turned, up halfway to the knees. This appearance is quite understandable if we suppose that the trousers were worn under a skirt and were turned up so that they should not be accidentally seen."

"Is it not rather strange," said Marchmont, "that Jeffrey should have allowed himself to be dressed up in this remarkable manner?"

"I think not," replied Thorndyke. "There is no reason to suppose that he knew how he was dressed. You have heard Jervis's description of his condition—that of a mere automaton. You know that without his spectacles he was practically blind, and that he could not have worn them since we found them at the house in Kennington Lane. Probably his head was wrapped up in the veil, and the skirt and mantle put on afterwards; but, in any case, his condition rendered him practically devoid of will power. That is all the evidence I have to prove that the unknown woman was Jeffrey. It is not conclusive, but

215

it is convincing enough for our purpose, seeing that the case against John Blackmore does not depend upon it."

"Your case against him is on the charge of murder, I presume?" said Stephen.

"Undoubtedly."

"Did you identify Mrs. Schallibaum?" asked Stephen. "You have told us nothing about her."

"I have considered her as being outside the case so far as I am concerned," replied Thorndyke. "She was an accessory; my business was with the principal. But, of course, she will be swept up in the net. The evidence that convicts John Blackmore will convict her. I have not troubled about her identity. If John Blackmore is married, she is probably his wife. Do you happen to know if he is married?"

"Yes, but Mrs. John Blackmore is not much like Mrs. Schallibaum, except that she has a cast in the left eye. She is a dark woman with very heavy eyebrows."

"That is to say that she differs from Mrs. Schallibaum in those peculiarities that can be artificially changed and resembles her in the one feature that is unchangeable. Do you know if her first name happens to be Pauline?"

"Yes, it is. She was a Miss Pauline Hagenbeck, a member of an American theatrical company. What made you ask?"

"The name which Jervis heard poor Jeffrey struggling to pronounce seemed to me to resemble Pauline more than any other name."

"There is one little point that strikes me," said Marchmont. "Is it not rather remarkable that the porter should have noticed no difference between the body of Jeffrey and the living man whom he knew by sight, and who must, after all, have been distinctly different in appearance?"

"I am glad you raised that question," Thorndyke replied, "for that very difficulty presented itself to me at the beginning of the case. But on thinking it over, I decided that it was an imaginary difficulty, assuming, as we do, that there was a good deal of resemblance between the two men. Put yourself in the porter's place and follow his mental processes. He is informed that a dead man is lying on the bed in Mr. Blackmore's rooms. Naturally, he assumes that the dead man is Mr. Blackmore. With this idea he enters the chambers and sees a man a good deal like Mr. Blackmore and wearing Mr. Blackmore's clothes, lying on Mr. Blackmore's bed. The idea that the body could be that of some other person has never entered his mind. If he notes any difference of appearance, he will put that down to the effects of death. I take it as evidence of great acuteness on the part of John Blackmore that he should have calculated so cleverly. For since the body was actually Jeffrey's, and was identified by the porter as that of his tenant, it has been assumed by every one that no question was possible as to the identity of Jeffrey Blackmore and the tenant of New Inn."

There was a brief silence, and then Marchmont asked, "May we take it that we have now heard all the evidence?"

"Yes," replied Thorndyke. "That is my case."

"Have you given information to the police?" Stephen asked eagerly.

"Yes. As soon as I had obtained the statement of the cabman, Ridley, and felt that I had enough evidence to secure a conviction, I called in at Scotland Yard and had an interview with the assistant commissioner. The case is in the hands of Superintendent Miller of the Criminal Investigation Department, a most acute and energetic officer. I have been expecting to hear that the warrant has been executed, for Mr. Miller is usually very punctilious in keeping me informed of the progress of the cases to which I introduce him. We shall hear tomorrow, no doubt."

"Well then, for the present," said Marchmont, "the case seems to have passed out of our hands."

"I shall enter a caveat, all the same," said Mr. Winwood.

"That doesn't seem very necessary," Marchmont objected. "The evidence that we have heard is amply sufficient to ensure a conviction, and there will be plenty more when the police go into the case. And a conviction on the charges of forgery and murder would, of course, invalidate the second will."

"Indeed it shall," agreed Mr. Winwood, "but I shall enter a caveat, just the same, to be sure that all matters are fully disposed."

As the two partners showed a disposition to become heated over this question, Thorndyke suggested that they might discuss it at leisure by the light of subsequent events. Acting on this hint—for it was now close upon midnight—our visitors took their leave.

"So you see, Jervis, why I never reject a case out of hand. The most unlikely case is at least worth thinking over."